Textbook written according to revised syllabus of F.Y.B.Com.
prescribed by University of Pune from 2013-2014.
Also useful for other universities in Maharashtra.

Business Economics

Prof. Vaishali Apte

Chartered Accountant

Visiting faculty,
Symbiosis Institute of Business Management (SIBM), Pune

Diamond Publication

Business Economics

Prof. Vaishali Apte

First Edition : June 2013

ISBN 978-81-8483-530-4

© **Diamond Publications**

Cover Page :
Sham Bhalekar

Published by :
Diamond Publications
264/3 Shaniwar Peth, 302 Anugrah Apartment
Near Omkareshwar Temple, Pune - 411 030
☎ 020-24452387, 24466642

info@diamondbookspune.com
www.diamondbookspune.com

Sale Distributor :
Diamond Book Depot
661 Narayan Peth
Appa Balwant Chowk
Pune 411 030
Tel. - 24480677, 66020282

Syllabus

University of Pune
(2013 - 14)
F.Y. B.Com.
Compulsory Paper
Subject Name -: Business Economics (Micro)

Objectives -:

1. To expose Students of Commerce to basic micro economic concepts and inculcate an analytical approach to the subject matter.
2. To stimulate the student interest by showing the relevance and use of various economic theories.
3. To apply economic reasoning to problems of business.

First Term

Unit No.   Topic

1.   INTRODUCTION.

1.1   Meaning, Nature and Scope of Business Economics- (Micro)

1.2   Difference between Micro and Macro Economics.

1.3   Tools for Analysis
        a. Functional Relationships
        b. Schedules
        c. Graphs
        d. Equations

1.4   Goals of firms
        a) Economic Goals of Firms
                1. Profit Maximization
                2. Shareholders Wealth Maximization
                3. Management Reward Maximization
                4. Growth of the firm
                5. Sales maximization
                6. Long run survival
        b) Non-Economic goals
                1. Political power, Prestige
                2. Social responsibility and welfare
                3. Goodwill of employees

2. DEMAND ANALYSIS

2.1 Elasticity of Demand, Types of Elasticity, Price Elasticity, Income Elasticity and Cross Elasticity.

2.2 Consumer Behaviour
a) Marginal Utility Approach
- Limitations
b) Indifference Curve Analysis
- Concept
- Characteristics
- Consumer Equilibrium

2.3 Demand Forecasting and Estimation
a) Meaning and objectives of Demand Forecasting
b) Methods of Demand Forecasting
c) Descriptive Analysis of
i) Direct Methods
1) Consumer Survey
2) Expert opinion
3) Simulating market situation
4) Controlled Market Experiments
ii) Indirect Methods
1) Simple correlation
2) Trend Projections

3. PRODUCTION AND COST ANALYSIS

3.1 Production Function – Meaning

3.2 Law of Variable Proportions - The Three Stages

3.3 Law of Returns to Scale - The Three Stages

3.4 Economies and Diseconomies of Scale – Internal and External

3.5 Cost Analysis – Types of Costs
a) Types of Costs
1) Total cost
2) Average Cost
3) Marginal Cost
4) Opportunity cost
b) Behaviour of Cost Curves
1) In the Short Run
2) In the Long Run

Second Term

Unit No.	Topic

4. REVENUE BEHAVIOUR
4.1 Meaning and Importance of Revenue Concepts
4.2 Total Revenue (TR), Average Revenue (AR)
Marginal Revenue (MR).
4.3 Relationship between Total Revenue, Average Revenue
and Marginal Revenue

5. PRICING UNDER VARIOUS MARKET CONDITIONS
5.1 Perfect Competition – Features and equilibrium
5.2 Monopoly – Features and equilibrium, Price Discrimination
5.3 Monopolistic competition - Features and equilibrium
5.4 Oligopoly – Features

6. FACTOR PRICING
6.1 Marginal Productivity theory of Distribution.
6.2 Rent
a) Theories of Rent
i) Ricardian Theory of Rent
ii) Modern Theory of Rent
6.3 WAGES -
i) Backward sloping Supply curve of Labour.
ii) Collective Bargaining & Trade Unions
6.4 INTEREST -
a) Theories of Interest –
i) Loanable Fund Theory of Interest
ii) Keynes Liquidity Preference Theory of Interest
6.5 PROFIT -
a) Theories of Profit –
i) Dynamic Theory of Profits
ii) Innovation Theory of Profit
iii) Risk and Uncertainty Theory of Profit

Contents

Part I

Part - II

Introduction to Business Economics

Contents

---

1 INTRODUCTION - MEANING NATURE AND SCOPE OF BUSINESS ECONOMICS

Knowledge of economics is useful in almost all spheres of life. Economics provides certain tools which can be used for solving various business problems. The knowledge about economic situation in the country and the world has a great bearing on the success of business.

Business economics is an integration of economic principles with business management practices It pertains to economic analysis that can be used in solving business problems, policy and planning .Economic theory with appropriate modifications can be used by the business firms to achieve their targets.

"Business Economics", according to **Malcolm McNair and Richard Meriam**, "consists of the use of economic modes of thought to analyse business situations".

Application of economic concepts to business realities is a major concern of Business Economics. In doing so, Business Economics uses the methodology of Economics. Predicting economic quantities like demand, profits, costs etc. is of vital importance for business community. In Economics various analytical tools and concepts are studied for this purpose. Economic theory with appropriate modifications can be used by the business firms to achieve the targets set by them.

Business economics seeks to establish rules and principles to enable business firms to achieve the economic goals of business management.

One of the major challenges faced by economic science is the optimum allocation of resources. Because resources are scarce, one must aim at making the best possible use of these resources. This is applicable, to a family, a nation or a firm. The management of any business unit obviously has to ensure such an optimum allocation of whatever human and material resources are available. Through its study of costs and its policies regarding profits and promotion of its products a firm must try to achieve this aim. Business Economics analyses the costs, assesses the market categories and tries to fit in its policies within the setting of macro-economic variables.

Business Economics is essentially applied micro-economics as the subject of study of Business Economics is a business firm. A business firm is the smallest decision-making unit on the side of production in the micro-economic theory. Hence problems facing the business firm are also within the area of Micro-Economics. For example, elasticity of demand or the techniques of demand forecasting are all matters of micro-economic study. Also,the pricing policies of the firms have to take into account various market structures within which it has to operate and a study of the market structures falls within the ambit of Micro Economics.

Hence, it would be clear that. Business Economics is basically concerned with what is known as the 'Theory of the Firm in Economics. In fact, Business Economics uses almost all the concepts and principles of the theory of the firm.

However, a firm has to operate within the macro-setting of a given economy. Its prospects are governed by the trends in aggregate income, in consumption patterns and in the investment and saving levels of the economy. The macro-policies can limit or can increase these prospects. Business Economics takes into its stride the nature and functioning of the macro-economy along with the policy instruments normally used by the government. BusinessEconomics, through its study of the economic environment and of macro-level planning, provides the basis for decision making. These decisions are taken scientifically.

Scope of Business Economics

The following areas can be said to constitute the scope of Business Economics.

(1) **Theory of consumer behavior :** Economics is a science of choice making. Scarcity of resources is a given condition. Ends are ulimited. A choice is required to be made and priorities are to be understood properly. Business Economics has to begin its study with an understanding of the basic economic problem. Demand analysis is an important area of scope of business economics which is closely related to the theory of consumer behaviour

(2) **Theory of the Firm :** An individual firm's price and output are determined under various market structures. The environment in which a firm operates is studied and is covered by the scope of business economics.

(3) **Theory of production :** Creating utility in a commodity is called production. Production function, Optimum product mix, Estimating cost of production, Profit planning , Law of Variable Proportions , Law of returns to Scale are studied under the scope of business economics.

(4) **Theory of costs :** The behavior of costs is governed by the cost-output relationship which varies from product to product and from one market condition to another. A variety of cost concepts like short-run and long-run costs is a part of the study of costs. An understanding of the factors causing variations in costs are of great relevance to the firms because they have to undertake cost forecasting for the purpose of planning. Moreover, there is a distinction between the economic costs and the accounting costs. Hence, cost concepts and their uses in decision-making, determinants of costs, break-even analysis and cost forecasting are some of the important topics included in Business Economics.

(5) **Theory of Pricing :** Price is the source of revenue to a firm. The extent to which the firm would be able control the price depends upon the type of market structure in which it is operating. The pricing practice followed by a firm would differ from firm to firm and from time to time in respect of the same firm. Pricing methods and problems of pricing are topics covered in business economics.

(6) **Theory of distribution :** Firms must know the issues involved in the pricing of factors of production. Factor remuneration is governed by a different set of conditions regarding its demand and supply. Theories of wage, Theories of rent, theories of profit and theories of interest are the areas of business economics.

(7) **Capital Management :** Firms require capital for various purposes. Capital base of any firm has to be sound. Capital planning is done from time to time by firms. Adequacy of capital is not a static concept which remains constant. It varies in different situations. Capital management is concerned with cost of capital and selection of appropriate projects.

(8) **Profit Management :** Success of a firm depends on the volume of profit. Various theories of profit, profit planning are studied under the scope of business economics.

(9) **Macro Economics :** The macroeconomic environment of business includes the general social and economic environment. It includes taxation, trade policies internal and

international, fiscal policy, monetary policy,industrial policy and situations related to changes in the levels of income and employment. Their study is important for business managers and it becomes the scope of business economics.

1.1 DIFFERENCE BETWEEN MICRO ECONOMICS AND MACRO ECONOMICS.

Micro-economics :

Micro stands for just a small part of the whole. In micro economics we analyse the part of a unit of the whole system. e.g, the behavior of an individual, firm or industry in the national economy. It tries to explain the behavior of individual consumer or the smallest unit of consumption, i.e. the household and individual producer or the smallest unit of production, i.e. the firm. The decisions regarding production and consumption taken by these producers and consumers add up to market supply and market demand respectively. On the assumption of the consumer's objectives of satisfaction-maximization, micro-economics studies the conditions of equilibrium of the consumer. Similarly, on the basis of the assumption of profit-maximization, macro-economic seeks to explain the equilibrium of the producer i.e. the firm and then the industry.

Through the interplay of the forces of demand and supply, prices of commodities and services are determined. As a result of the interplay of these forces, decisions regarding 'what to produce' and how much to produce are taken. Guided by the profit-motive, producers try to produce things in the most economical way and this answers the question 'how to produce'. This whole process is the subject matter for micro-economics.

Along with the product market, the study of the factor market is also undertaken by micro-economics. Scarcity of resources makes it necessary to ensure that resources are used in the best possible manner.

It will thus be clear that study of microeconomics covers Consumer behaviour,Product pricing,factor pricing and study of firms.

MACRO-ECONOMICS

Macro Economics : It is aggregative economics wherein the overall conditions of the economy such as total production, total consumption,total savings and total investment are studied. Macro economics includes study of national income and output, balance of trade and payments, general price level, external value of money, saving and investment, employment and economic growth.

Distinction between micro and macro economics is not clear-cut. What is macro from national stand point is micro in the world context. Similarly what is micro from a national angle becomes macro from a regional angle. In most of the cases both micro and macro economics play a complementary role e.g. national income cannot grow unless the production in individual firms rises. But in some cases, such a complementary role is not there, e.g. an increase in personal savings of a section of people may not lead to an increase in the savings of the community as a whole. Also a general rise in the price level has varying effect on different sections of the community. Hence study of both micro and macro economics is essential.

1.2 TOOLS FOR ANALYSIS

i) *Functional relationship :* Functional relation is a matheniatical expression showing relationship belween any two variables. It is useful for economic theory where we are required to study several relations like price and supply, demand and price, consumption and income, rate of interest and money supply and so on.

Functional relationship can be symbolically expressed as:

$$Qd = f(p)$$

Where   Qd   = Quantity demanded
          f   = Functinal relationship
          p   = Price

This means the Qd is a function of (p). The relationship between the variables such as demand and income or demand and price is called as functional relationship. It can be direct or inverse. Price and supply are directly related.

ii) *Schedules :* Functional relationship between any two variables indicates that the value of a dependent variable varies directly or inversely with the changes in the value of the independent variable. A schedule expresses the values of the dependent variables in response to the changes in the values of the independent variable.

In mathematical terms, it may be stated as:

$$Y = f(x)$$

Where, f stands for "a function of". This means that Y is a function of X that is to say, Y is related to X.

Table-Schedule

X	Y
1	6
2	7
3	8
4	9
5	10

On the basis of this function, we can construct the tabular sequence of Y values for alternative specified values of X. Such a table is called as schedule.

iii) *Graphs :* Generally, graph is a diagram showing, variation of two quantities, can be of curved lines. Vertical and horizontal are common in statistics and Geography. A graphical representation of above demand schedule is shown below:

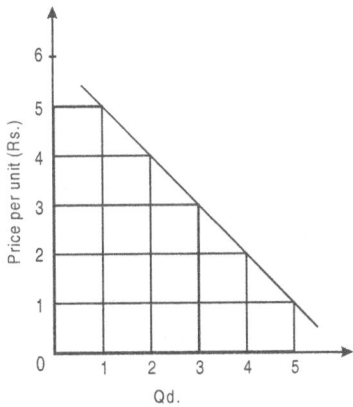

Figure 1.1

This is an income equation where total income (Y) is earned from production activities of two goods, consumption goods *(C)* and investment or capital goods (I).

$$Y = C + S$$

This is an expenditure equation where total income (Y) is spent partly on consumption goods (C) and partly left unconsumed i.e. saved (S).

iv) *Equations :* Equations represents the relationship between the values of dependent and independent variables. Identities are always true for all possible values of the variable. Thus equations help us to explain certain of the variable Hypothesis that of identities are just tautology and are always true e.g.

$$a^2 = a \times a \text{ or } (a + b)^2 = a^2 + 2ab + b^2$$

1.3 GOALS OF FIRMS

Business Economics deals with business firms. Therefore, it is necessary to understand the concept of business firm and its objectives. We may define a 'firm' as an organization engaged in the production of goods and services, which directly or indirectly help people in satisfying their various wants. All these firms are engaged in the production and exchange of goods and services. It means, all institutions engaged in either production or exchange may be called firms. All these firms mobilize money use that money to bring together men and material, direct production of goods and services and sell them in return for money.

Secondly, all firms are classified into two groups.

Private Business firms.

Nonprofit organization.

Econcmic Goals *or* objectives

i) Profit maximization.

ii) Shareholders wealth maximization.

iii) Management reward or utility maximization.

iv) Growth of the firm.

v) Sales maximization.

vi) Long-run survival.

i) Profit maximization: Conventional theory of firm assumes profit maximization as the sole objective of business firms.

All business firms have some organizational goals to pursue. The best way to find out the common objective of business firms would be to ask the business executives. Profit maximization is regarded as the most common and theoretically objective of business firms. In this section, we describe the conditions of profit maximization and the controversy on profit maximization as the objective of business firms.

Profit Maximizing Conditions

TotaProfit (II) defined as

$$II = TR - TC$$

Where TR = Total Revenue

TC = Total Cost

There are two conditions that must be fulfilled for TR - TC to be maximum. These conditions are called

a. Necessary Condition

b. Secondary Supplementary Condition.

The two conditions are also called the first order and the 'second order' conditions.

The necessary or the first order condition requires that for profit to be maximum marginal revenue (MR) must be equal to marginal cost (MC), i.e. MR = MC. By definition, marginal revenue is the revenue obtained from the production and sale of one additional unit of output and marginal cost arising due to the production of one additional unit of output.

The secondary or the second order condition required that the necessary condition must be satisfied under the condition of decreasing MR and rising MC. The fulfillment of the two conditions is make the sufficient condition.

This conditions illustrated by P_2 in the following diagram:

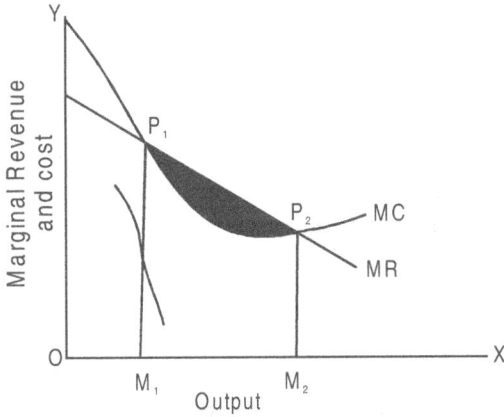

Figure 1.2

Arguments in Favour of profit Maximization Hypothesis

a) *Profit is indispensable for firm's survival :* The survival of all profit oriented firms in the long run depends on their ability to make a reasonable profit depending on'the business conditions and the level of competition. Making profit is a necessary condition for the survival of the firm. Once the firms are able to make profit, they try to make it as large as possible, i.e. they tend to maximize it.

b) *Achieving other objectives depends on firm's ability to make profit :* Many other objectives of business firms have been given in economic literature e.g., maximization of long-run growth, maximization of sales revenue, satisfying all the concerned parties, increasing and retaining market share etc. The achievement of such alternative objectives depends wholly or partly on the primary objective of making profit.

c) *Evidence against profit maximization objective not conclusive :* Profit maximization is a time-honoured objective of business firms. The evidence against it is not conclusive.

d) *Profit maximization objective has a greater predicting power :* The ultimate test of its validity is its ability to predict the business behaviour and the business trends.

e) *Profit is a more reliable measure of firm's efficiency :* Though not perfect, profit is the most efficient and reliable measure of the efficiency of a firm. It is also the source of internal finance. Profit as a source of internal finance assumes a greater significance when financial market is highly volatile.

ii) Shareholders wealth maximization objective : The objective of any business firm should be to maximize its wealth and value of the shares of the company. This objective is also termed as maximization of value

Wealth maximization objective as decision criteria suggests that any financial action which creates wealth or which has discounted stream of future benefits exceeding its cost, is desirable and should be accepted and that which does not satisfy this test should be rejected.

Following are the major elements of the strategy to maximise wealth of shareholders.

a) Many of the consumer products and almost all producers goods are purchased on the merit of their quality. Branding of products helps to impress upon the customers the brand quality association. It also helps to create a brand-loyalty.

b) The core business of the firm remains of vital importance. It must be strengthened through measures aimed at rationalization, cost effectiveness, quality control and widening of capital base.

c) All products, processes, procedures and personnel are subjected to continuous scrutiny for finding output where and how the cost of production can be reduced.

d) A sense of partnership has got be created in the minds of customers, distribution, sales force and retailers. Several schemes of doing this can be and are devised by modern firms.

e) Sustained long-term growth is a major parameter for ensuring the growth of shareholders wealth. This is discussed in detail below.

iii) Management reward maximisation objective : Utility or satisfaction remains end objective of human behaviour. In case of small firms where the entrepreneur is owner as well as manager of the firm pursues the objective of utility maximization. The satisfaction to the entrepreneur does not come only from the maximization of profit but he may get this satisfaction from the leisure which he is able to enjoy.

iv) Growth of the firm objective : Managers pursue not single but multiple goal such as sales maximization, utility maximization etc. Along with these objectives, managers keep the prime objectives to achieve the top level or the highest possible level of growth in output they also try to improve their prestige, technical superiority and market power. They take the help of an effective advertising on large scale influence the consumers in order to attain the above said objective.

Actually, it can be treated as separate objectives of a firm. This is because when the profits increase or sales increase, firm earns more and grows in size. Growth of a firm can be vertical or horizontal. Expansion diversifications are the indicators of growth of firm. Growth indicates success of the firm. In order to get the advantage of internal economies, firm aims at its growth. Acquisition or merger may help the firm to grow in the era of globalization.

v) Sales maximisation objective: According to Prof. Baumal the ultimate objective of firm is sales maximization rather than profit maximization. He opines that sales have become an end of themselves i.e. of firms.

Thus, he thinks that sales maximization is a prime objective of the firm. He further says that sales refers to the revenue earned by selling the product. He calls it as sales maximization hypothesis or the 'revenue maximization hypothesis'.

He points out that in the practical word businessman usually promotes sales, subject to the limitation that cost incurred are covered and usual rate of returns are secured. Thus, the firm will try to attain the minimum level of profit after which sales rather than profit becomes the overriding objective of the firm.

vi) Long run survival goal : The primary objective of every firm is to survive its business in the long-term. For ensuring long-run. Survival the firm will have to implement various policy measures, such as delivering quality product, adopting competitive pricing strategy, providing higher level of consumer satisfaction, adopting cost control techniques etc.

Non-Economic Goals

i) *Political power prestige :* Successful large business firms enjoy tremendous .prestige in the society. Such business firms influences the government decision, governments, economic policies, etc. considerably to its advantage. So for every business firm, achieving significant political power and prestige is its prominent non economic goal.

ii) *Social responsibility and welfare:* Social responsibility and welfare constitute one of the prominent non-economic goal of business firm-social responsibility requires an organization to meet the expectations norms and values of society. Business firms, besides earning profits cater to the social needs of various sections of the society.

iii) *Goodwill of employees:* Every business firm tries to satisfy its employees, happy employees (i.e. human resource) is a very valuable asset for any business firm. For achieving maximum goodwill for the benefit of employees the firm has to provide various monetary and non-monetary incentives to the employees, viz. hike in salaries, hike in dearness allowance, free educational loan house rent allowance, free medical treatment and many more.

Exercise

1. What is Business Economics? Explain the scope of Business Economics.
2. Explain the various economic Goals of business firm.
3. Explain the Non-Economic goals of Business firm.
4. Explain the various tools for analysis.

CHAPTER
2

Demand

Contents

2.0 INTRODUCTION

Market mechanism depends on the forces of demand and supply. Demand analysis is concerned with the economic activities of a consumer i.e consumption. In market mechanism, the function of price determination is done by both the forces of demand and supply. Demand analysis has been used most extensively in business.

2.1 CONCEPT OF DEMAND

The concept 'demand' refers to the quantity of a good or service that consumers are willing and able to purchase at various prices during a period of time. Demand in economics is something more than desire to purchase though desire is one element of it. A beggar, for instance, may desire food, but due to lack of means to purchase it, his demand is not effective. Thus effective demand for a thing depends on

(i) desire

(ii) means to purchase and

(iii) on willingness to use those means for that purchase.

Unless demand is backed by purchasing power or ability to pay, it does not constitute demand. Quantity demanded is always expressed at a given price. At different prices different quantities of a commodity are generally demanded. Also quantity demanded is a flow. We are concerned not with a single isolated purchase, but with a continuous flow of purchases and we must therefore express demand as so much per period of time.

Factors determining Demand : There are a number of factors which influence household demand for a commodity, important among these are:

(i) Price of the commodity,

(ii) Prices of other related commodities,

(iii) Level of income of the household,

(iv) Tastes and preferences of consumers,

(v) Size and composition of population,

(vi) Distribution of income,

(vii) Other factors.

The above listed factors can easily be presented in the form of a demand function as follows:

$$Q_{dc} = f(P_c, P_r, Y, T, D)$$

where Q_{dc} is the quantity demanded of commodity c, P_C is the price of commodity, c, P_r is the price of related commodities, Y is the money income of the household, T is the taste of the household, and D represents size of the population and other remaining factors.

(i) Price of the commodity: Ceteris paribus i.e. other things being equal; the demand of a commodity is inversely related to its price. It implies that a rise in price of a commodity brings about a fall in its purchase and vice-versa. This happens because of income and substitution effects.

(ii) Price of related commodities: Related commodities are of two types: (a) complementary goods and (ii) competing goods or substitutes. Complementary goods are those goods which are consumed together or simultaneously. For example, tea and sugar, automobiles and petrol, pen and ink are used together. When commodities are complements, a fall in the price of one (other things being equal) will cause the demand of the other to rise. For example, a fall in the price of cars would lead to a rise in the demand for petrol. Similarly, a fall in the price of pens will cause a rise in the demand for ink. The reverse will be the case when the price of a complement rises.

Competing goods or substitutes are those goods which can be used with ease in place of one another. For example, tea and coffee, ink pen and ball pen, are substitutes for each other and can be used in place of, one another easily. When goods are substitutes, a fall in the price of one (ceteris paribus) leads to a fall in the quantity demanded of its substitutes. For example, if the price of tea falls, people will try to substitute it for coffee and demand more of it and less of coffee i.e. the demand for tea will rise and that of coffee fall.

(iii) Level of income of the household: Other things being equal, the demand for a commodity depends upon the money income of the household. In most cases, the larger the average money income of the household, the larger is the quantity demanded of a particular good. However, there are certain commodities for which quantities demanded decrease with an increase in money income. These goods are called *inferior goods.* Even in the case of other goods, the response of quantities demanded to changes in their prices is not of same proportions. If goods are such that they satisfy the basic necessities (food, clothing, shelter) of life a change in their prices although will cause an increase in demand for these necessities this increase will be less than proportionate to the increase in income This is because as people become richer, there is a relative decline in importance of food and other non durable goods in the overall consumption pattern and a rise in importance of durable goods such as a TV, car, house etc.

(iv) Tastes and preferences of consumers: The demand for a commodity also depends upon tastes and preferences of consumers and changes in them over a period of time. Goods which are more in fashion command higher demand than goods which are out of fashion.

(v) Other factors: Apart from the above factors, the demand for a commodity depends upon the following factors:

    (a) *Size of population:* Generally, larger the size of population of a country or a region, greater is the demand for commodities in general.

    (b) *Composition of population:* If there are more old people in a region, the demand for spectacles, walking sticks, etc. will be high. Similarly, if the population consists of more of children, demand for toys, baby foods, choclates, will be more.

    (c) *Distribution of Income:* The wealth of a country may be so distributed that there are a few exceptionally rich people while the majority are exceedingly poor. Under such conditions the propensity to consume of the country will be relatively less, for the propensity to consume of the rich people is less than that of the poor people. Consequently, the demand for consumer goods will be comparatively less. If the distribution of income is more equal, then the propensity to consume of the country as a whole will be relatively high indicating higher demand for goods.

Apart from above, factors such as class, group, education, marital status consumer's expectations with regard to future price and weather conditions, also play an important role in influencing household demand.

2.2 LAW OF DEMAND

The law of demand is one of the most important laws of economic theory. According to law of demand, other things being equal, if the price of a commodity falls, the quantity demanded of it will rise and if the price of a commodity rises, its quantity demanded will decline. Thus, there is an inverse relationship between price and quantity demanded, other things being same. The other things which are assumed to be equal or constant are the prices of related commodities, income of consumers, tastes and preferences of consumers, and such other factors which influence demand. If these factors which determine demand also undergo a change, then the inverse price-demand relationship may not hold good. For example, if incomes of consumers increase, then an increase in the price of a commodity, may not result in a decrease in the quantity demanded of it.

Exceptions to the Law of Demand :

According to the law of demand, more of a commodity will be demanded at lower prices than at higher prices, other things being equal. The law of demand is valid in most of the cases; however there are certain cases where this law does not hold good. The following are the important exceptions to the law of demand.

(i) *Conspicuous goods:* Some consumers measure the utility of a commodity by its price i.e. if the commodity is expensive they think that it has got more utility. As such, they buy less of this commodity at low price and more of it at high price. Diamonds are often given as example of this case. Higher the price of diamonds, higher is the prestige value attached to them and hence higher is the demand for them.

(ii) *Giffen goods:* Sir Robert Giffen, an economist, was surprised to find out that as the price of bread increased, the British workers purchased more bread and not less of it. This was something against the law of demand. Why did this happen? The reason given for this is that when the price of bread went up, it caused such a large decline in the purchasing power of the poor people that they were forced to cut down the consumption of meat and other more expensive foods. Since bread even when its price was higher than before was still the cheapest food article, people consumed more of it and not less when its price went up.

Such goods which exhibit direct price-demand relationship are called 'Giffen goods'. Generally those goods which are considered inferior by the consumers and which occupy a substantial place in consumer's budget are called 'Giffen goods'. Examples of such goods are coarse grains like bajra, low quality of rice and wheat etc.

(iii) *Conspicuous necessities:* The demand for certain goods is affected by the demonstration effect of the consumption pattern of a social group to which an individual belongs. These goods, due to their constant usage, have become necessities of life. For example, in spite of the fact that the prices of television sets, refrigerators, coolers, cooking gas etc. have been continuously rising, their demand does not show any tendency to fall.

(iv) *Future expectations about prices:* It has been observed that when the prices are rising, households expecting that the prices in the future will be still higher tend to buy larger quantities of the commodities. For example, when there is wide-spread drought, people expect that prices of food grains would rise in future. They demand greater quantities of food grains as their price rise. But it is to be noted that here it is not the law of demand which is invalidated but there is a change in one of the factors which was held constant while deriving the law of demand, namely change in the price expectations of the people.

(v) The law has been derived assuming consumers to be rational and knowledgeable about market-conditions. However, at times consumers tend to be irrational and make impulsive purchases without any cool calculations about price and usefulness of the product and in such contexts the law of demand fails.

(vi) Similarly, in practice, a household may demand larger quantity of a commodity even at a higher price because it may be ignorant of the ruling price of the commodity. Under such circumstances, the law will not remain valid.

2.3 ELASTICITY OF DEMAND

Definition :

Elasticity of demand is defined as the responsiveness of the quantity demanded of a good to changes in one of the variables on which demand depends or we can say that it is the percentage change in quantity demanded divided by the percentage in one of the variables on which demand depends. These variables are price of the commodity, prices of the related commodities, income of the consumers and other various factors on which demand depends. Thus we have *price elasticity, cross elasticity, elasticity of substitution and income elasticity.* It is price elasticity of demand which is usually referred to as elasticity of demand.

Price Elasticity :

Price elasticity of demand expresses the response of quantity demanded of a good to a change in its price, given the consumer's income, his tastes and prices of all other goods. In other words, it is measured as percentage change in quantity demanded divided by the percentage change in price, other things remaining equal. That is

$$\text{Price Elasticity} = E_P = \frac{\% \text{ Change in quantity demanded}}{\% \text{ Change in Price}}$$

OR

$$E_P = \frac{\text{Change in Quantity}}{\text{Original Quantity}} \times \frac{\text{Original Price}}{\text{Change in Price}}$$

$$E_P = \frac{\Delta q}{q} \times \frac{p}{\Delta p} = \frac{\Delta q}{\Delta p} \times \frac{p}{q}$$

Where Ep stands for price elasticity

    q stands for quantity

    p stands for price

    A stands for a very small change.

The value of price elasticity varies from minus infinitely to approach zero from the negative sign, because $\dfrac{\Delta q}{\Delta p}$ has a negative sign. In other words, since price and quantity are inversely related (with a few exceptions) price elasticity is negative. But for the sake of convenience, we ignore the negative sign and consider only the numerical value of the elasticity. Thus if a 1% change in price leads to 2% change in quantity demanded of good A and 4% change in quantity demanded of good B, then we get elasticity of A and B as 2 and 4 respectively, showing that demand for B is more elastic or responsive to price changes than A. Had we considered minus signs, we would have concluded that A is more elastic than B, which is not correct. Hence by convention we take absolute value of price elasticity and draw conclusions.

Methods of Measuring Price elasticity of Demand

1) Point elasticity : In point elasticity, we measure elasticity at a given point on a demand curve. Point elasticity makes use of derivative rather than finite changes in price and quantity. It may be defined as:

$$\frac{-dq}{dp} \times \frac{p}{p}$$

where $\dfrac{dq}{dp}$ is the derivative of quantity with respect to price at a point on the demand curve, and p and q are the price and quantity at that point.

Thus given the demand function, elasticity at any point can be found by using the above formula. For example, with the demand function $Qd= 1000 - 10p2$, the elasticity at $P = 5$ (Rs.) is calculated as follows:

$$\frac{dq}{dp} = -20p$$

when p = 5, the quantity demanded is 750. Therefore,

$$Ep = -20(5) \times \frac{5}{750} = -66.$$

It is to be noted that elasticity is different at different points on the same demand curve. Given a straight line demand curve tT, point elasticity at any point say R can be found by using formula*

$$\frac{RT}{Rt} = \frac{\text{lower segment}}{\text{upper segment}}$$

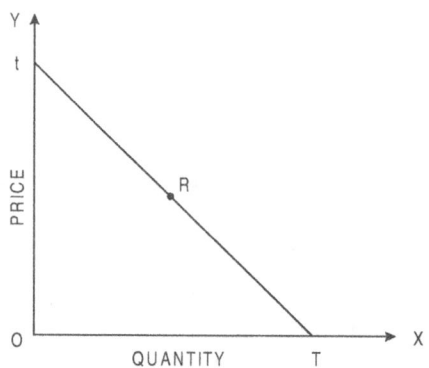

Fig. 2.1: Elasticity at a point on the demand curve

Using the above formula we can get elasticity at various points on the demand curve.

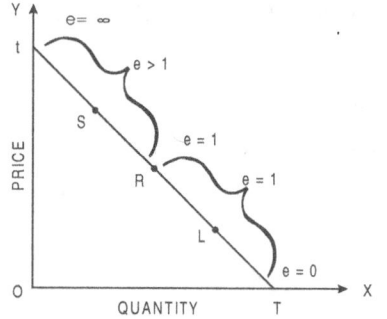

Fig. 2.2(i) : Elasticity at different points on a demand curve

Fig. 2.2 (ii) : Arc Elasticity

We will get something like given in Figure 2.2 (i).

Thus we see that as we move from T towards *t*, elasticity goes on increasing. At the mid-point it is equal to one, at *t* it is infinity and at *T* it is zero.

II) Arc-elasticity : When the price change is some what larger or when price elasticity is to be found between the txwo prices [or two points on the demand curve say A and B in figure (ii)], the question arise which price and quantity should be taken as base. This is because elasticities found by using original price and quantity figures as base will be different from the one derived by using new price and quantity figures. Therefore, in order to avoid confusion, generally averages of the two prices and quantities are taken as (i.e. original and new) base. The arc elasticity can be found out by using the formula:

$$Ep = \frac{\Delta q}{\Delta p} \times \frac{\frac{p_1 + p_2}{2}}{\frac{q_1 + q_2}{2}} \quad OR \quad Ep = \frac{\Delta q}{\Delta p} \times \frac{p_1 + p_2}{q_1 + q_2}$$

OR

$$Ep = \frac{p_1 - p_2}{q_1 + q_2} \times \frac{p_1 + p_2}{q_1 + q_2}$$

where p_1, q_1 are the original price and quantity and p_2, q_2 are the new ones.

Thus if we have to find elasticity of radios between:

$$P_1 = Rs. 500 \qquad q_1 = 100$$
$$P_2 = RS. 400 \qquad q_2 = 150$$

We will use the formula

$$Ep = \frac{q_1 - q_2}{q_1 + q_2} \times \frac{p_1 + p_2}{p_1 - p_2}$$

OR $\qquad Ep = \dfrac{50}{250} \times \dfrac{900}{100}$

OR $\qquad Ep = 1.8$

Interpreting numerical values of elasticity of demand

The numerical value of elasticity of demand can assume any value between zero and infinity.

Elasticity is zero, if there is no change at all in quantity demanded when price changes i.e. when quantity demanded does not respond to a price change.

Elasticity is one, or unitary, if the percentage change in quantity demanded is equal to the percentage change in price.

Elasticity is greater than one when the percentage change in quantity demanded is greater than the percentage change in price. In such a case, demand is said to be elastic.

Elasticity is less than one when the percentage change in quantity demanded is less than the percentage change in price. In such a case demand is said to be inelastic.

Elasticity is infinite, when some 'small price reduction raises the demand from zero to infinity. Under such a case consumers will buy all that they can obtain of the commodity at some price. If there is a slight increase in price, they would not buy anything from the particular seller. This type of demand curve is found in perfectly competitive market.

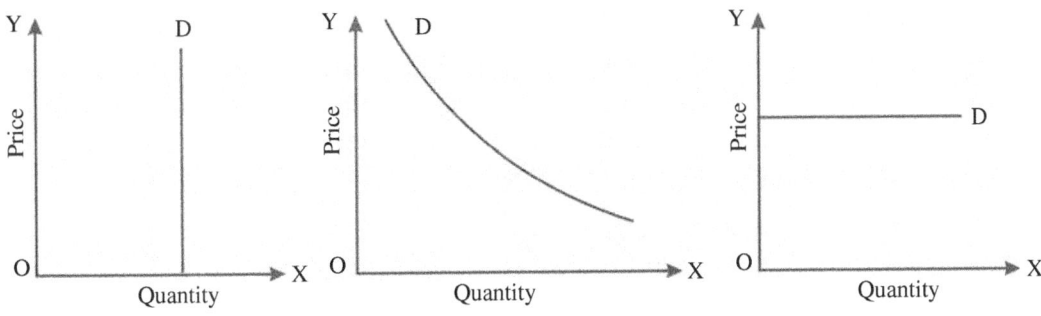

Fig. 2.3 : Demand curve of zero, unitary, and infinite elasticity

Table 2.1 : Elasticity measures, meaning and nomenclature

Numerical measure of elasticity	Verbal description	Terminology
Zero	Quantity demanded does not change as price changes	Perfectly (or completely) inelastic
Greater than zero, but less than one	Quantity demanded changes by a smaller percentage than does price	Inelastic
One	Quantity demanded changes by exactly the same percentage as does price	Unit elasticity
Greater than one, but less than infinity	Quantity demanded changes by a larger percentage than does price.	Elastic
Infinity	Purchasers are prepared to buy all they can obtain at some price and none at all at an even slightly higher price	Perfectly (or infinitely) elastic

iii) Total Outlay Method of calculating price elasticity : The price elasticity of demand for a commodity and the total expenditure or outlay made on it are greatly related to each other. By analysing the changes in total expenditure or outlay we can know the price elasticity of demand for the good. However, by this method we can only say whether a good is elastic or inelastic; we cannot find out the exact coefficient of elasticity.

When as a result of the change in price of a good; the total expenditure on the good remains the same, the price elasticity for the good is equal to unity. This is because total expenditure made on the good can remain the same only if the proportional change in quantity demanded is equal to the proportional change in price. Thus if there is a 100% increase in price of a good and if the price elasticity is unitary, total expenditure of the buyer on the good will remain unchanged.

When as a result of increase in price of a good, total expenditure made on the good falls or when as a result of decrease in price, the total expenditure made on the good increases, we say that price elasticity of demand is greater than unity.

When as a result of increase in price of a good, the total expenditure made on the good increases or when as a result of decrease in price, the total expenditure made on the good falls, we say that price elasticity of demand is less than unity.

Determinants of Price Elasticity of Demand

Following are the important determinants of price elasticity.

(1) *Availability of substitutes:* One of the most important determinants of elasticity is the degree of availability of close substitutes. Some commodities like butter, cabbage, Maruti,

Coca Cola, have close substitutes - margarine, other green vegetables, Fiat or other cars, Pepsi or any other cold drink. A change in price of these commodities, the prices of the substitutes remaining constant, can be expected to cause quite substantial substitution - a fall in price leading consumers to buy more of the commodity in question and a rise in price leading consumers to buy more of the substitutes. Other commodities such as salt, housing, and all vegetables taken together, have few, if any, satisfactory substitutes and a rise in their prices may cause a smaller fall in their quantity demanded. Thus we can say that goods which typically have close or perfect substitutes have highly elastic demand curves. It should be noted that while as a group a good or service may have inelastic demand, but when we consider its various brands, we say that a particular brand has elastic demand Thus while demand for petrol is inelastic, the demand for Indian Oil's petrol is elastic. Similarly, while there are no general substitutes for health care, there are substitutes for one doctor or for a nurse. Likewise, the demand for common salt is inelastic because good substitutes for common salt are not available.

(2) *Position of a commodity in a consumer's budget:* The greater the proportion of income spent on a commodity, the greater will be generally its elasticity of demand and vice-versa. The demand for goods like common salt, matches, buttons, etc. tend to be highly inelastic because a households spend only a fraction of their income on each of them. On the other hand, demand for goods like clothing, tends to be elastic since households generally spend a good part of their income on clothing.

(3) *Nature of the need that a commodity satisfies:* In general, luxury goods are price elastic while necessities are price inelastic. Thus while the demand for television is relatively elastic the demand for food and housing, in general, is inelastic.

(4) *Number of uses to which a commodity can be put:* The more the possible uses of a commodity the greater will be its price elasticity and vice versa. To illustrate, milk has several uses. If its price falls, it can be used for a variety of purposes like preparation of curd, cream, ghee and sweets. But if its price increases, its use will be restricted only to essential purposes like feeding the children and sick persons.

(5) *The period:* The longer the time-period one has, the more completely one can adjust. A homely example of the effect can be seen in motoring habits. In response to a higher petrol price, one can, in the short run, make fewer trips by car. In the longer run not only can one make fewer trips but he can purchase a car with a smaller engine capacity when the time comes for replacing the existing one. Hence one's demand for petrol falls by more when one has made long term adjustment to higher prices.

(6) *Consumer habits:* If a consumer is a habitual consumer of a commodity no matter how much its price change, the demand for the commodity will be inelastic.

(7) *Tied demand:* The demand for those goods which are tied to others is normally inelastic as against those whose demand is of autonomous nature.

(3) *Price range:* Goods which are in very high range or in very low price range have inelastic demand but those in the middle range have elastic demand.

Income-Elasticity of Demand

As indicated in the beginning, we can now switch over to another determinant of demand viz. income and consider elasticity of demand by holding all other determinants, including price, constant. Income-elasticity of demand for a product shows the extent to which a consumer's demand for that product changes consequent upon a change in his income. Income-elasticity of demand can be defined as the *ratio of proportionate change in the quantity demanded of the commodity to a given proportionate change in income of the consumer.* The formulae for measuring income-elasticity of demand can be stated, thus :

[A] Measurement of Income-Elasticity

Formula 1 :

$$E_y = \frac{\text{Proportionate change in quantity demanded}}{\text{Proportionate change in consumer's income}}$$

Example : A 20% rise in income causes a 30% increase in demand for a product 'X', what will be the income-elasticity of demand for 'X' ?

Solution : According to formula mentioned above :

$$E_y = \frac{30}{20} = 1.5$$

Formula 2 : A second formula which is mathematically more rational is suggested as under:

$$E_y = \frac{Q_2 - Q_1}{Q_2 + Q_1} \div \frac{Y_2 - Y_1}{Y_2 + Y_1}$$

In this formula, Q_1 is the initial consumer expenditure on any commodity 'X' (which represents the demand for the product 'X') and Q2 is the new expenditure on the same commodity after a change in income. Y_1 denotes initial income and Y_2 stands for or new income.

Example : A consumer spends Rs. 60 per month on sugar when his income is Rs. 1500 per month. When his income increases to Rs. 1800 per month, he spends Rs. 84. What will be the income-elasticity of demand for sugar in this case ?

Solution : According to the above formula :

$$E_y = \frac{84 - 60}{84 + 60} \div \frac{1800 - 1500}{1800 + 1500}$$

$$E_y = \frac{24}{144} \div \frac{300}{3300}$$

$$= \frac{1}{6} \div \frac{1}{11}$$

$$= \frac{11}{6} \text{ or } 1.8$$

Income-elasticity of demand in this case is 1.8.

Types of Income-Elasticity of Demand

According to the value of income-elasticity of demand, we can classify income-elasticity into the following five types :

1. *Negative Income-Elasticity :* When the demand for a product decreases as income increases and conversely when demand for a product increases as there is fall in income, the income elasticity of demand is negative. The demand for inferior goods is of this type.

2. *Zero Income-Elasticity :* When a change in income has no effect upon the quantity demanded of a product, the income-elasticity of demand would be zero. Demand for salt is an example of this type.

3. *Unit Income-Elasticity :* Income-elasticity of demand will be equal to unity (i.e. 1) when demand for the product increases in the same proportion in which income increases. Unit elasticity of demand is considered to be a dividing line between necessaries and comforts: In other words, the income elasticity of demand for necessaries will be less than unity : while the income elasticity of the demand for comforts will be more than unity. Both these cases are noted below.

4. *Low Income-Elasticity of demand :* When the income elasticity of demand for a product is positive i.e. greater than zero, but less than one, we say that the income elasticity of that demand is relatively less. Such a variety of relatively less income-elasticity or income-in elasticity of demand suggests that the commodity concerned must be a necessary. This is because as income increases the percentage of income spent on necessaries goes on diminishing, according to Engel's Law of family expenditure.

5. *High Income-Elasticity :* As opposed to the.above category, we get high income elasticity of demand for products which satisfy the consumers' comforts and luxuries. In other words, the income elasticity of demand for articles of comforts and luxuries is greater than unity.

The income elasticity for different products differs widely. Income-elasticity of demand tends to be very high in respect of luxury articles like gold, jewellery, precious stones, paintings, cars etc: As against this, income elasticity of demand is very low in commodities like salt, vanaspati, matches, kerosene, washing soap etc. Besides of a commodity i.e. whether it is a necessary or comfort or luxury, the proportion of consumers income spent on the commodity is also a major factor influencing income city of demand.

Uses of the Concept of Income-Elasticity of Demand

The concept of income-elasticity of demand is useful in many areas of economic policy-formulations as well as analysis of various situations.

1. *Economic Development :* In case of economic development, when national income is increasing, we can find out how much will be the increase in the demand for a given product by

considering the income-elasticity of demand for that product. Economic Fluctuations : Economic fluctuations are a characteristic feature of a capitalist economy. Phases of prosperity and depression alternate in such an economy. The concept of income-elasticity can be a very useful guide in finding out what products are demanded during the phase of prosperity. Similarly, during the phase of depression certain necessaries will continue to be demanded. As noted above, necessaries are commodities with very low income-elasticities.

3. 'Economic Planning : The concept of income-elasticity of demand is of great help to the planners who are planning for the economy as a whole. When economic development is being planned, the planners have to set targets of production in terms of physical quantities for various sectors of the economy. With the help of income-elasticity, the planners can estimate the possible increase in demand for the product, as a result of the targeted rate of growth of the economy. This would make the physical targets more realistic and would serve to maintain physical balances - a difficult task for the planners.

4. Demand forecasting : Firms are required to forecast the demand for their product. With the help of statistical information regarding trends in-growth of income as well as changes of distribution of income, the firm can forecast the demand for its product by using income-elasticity of demand for that product as a guide.

5. Foreign Trade : In the area of foreign trade, a country needs to take into account the income-elasticity of demand for its imports as well as exports. A country exporting agricultural products and articles of necessity faces an income-inelastic demand, compared to a country which is exporting articles of luxury. This difference influences terms of trade. Income-elasticity of demand serves as a guide in the matter of balance of payments disequilibrium also. For example, India has been an exporter of jute, tea, coffee, and spices; but the demand for all these commodities is income-inelastic. The rate of growth of India's exports therefore has remained relatively low. As against this, India's demand for imports like electronics, machinery, consumer durable etc. is income-elastic. Consequently, the rate of growth of India's imports has remained high. Thus we have been facing the problem of an increasing trade deficit in India during the last few years.

The list of areas where income-elasticity of demand is useful can be increased further by mentioning public finance, labour policy, industrial policy, etc. where the concept is useful.

Cross-Elasticity of Demand

In practice, commodities are seldom independent of one another. Among the wide range of products that we see at the market, we find that most of these goods are related. On the basis of the relationship, we can group these products either as substitutes or as complements or as a third group of goods which are neutral. In the context of the relationship between goods, the concept of cross-elasticity of demand can be used. Cross elasticity of demand may be defined as the *ratio of proportionate change of quantity demanded of commodity 'X' to a given proportionate change in price of the related commodity 'Y'.* With the help of formula, similar to the one we noted earlier, we can say :

$$E_C = \frac{\text{Percentage change in quantity demanded of 'X'}}{\text{Percentage change in the price of 'Y'}}$$

If we assume the two commodities X and Y are substitutes of that each other and that 1 price of Y rises but that of X remains constant, the quantity demanded of X will increas because the consumers will now substitute X for Y, since Y has become costlier. Conversely, if the price of Y falls leaving the price of X unchanged, the quantity demanded of X will decrease because the consumers will now substitute Y for X since Y has become cheaper than before.

Cross elasticity can also be measured by another formula as given below

$$E_c = \frac{\dfrac{QX_2 - QX_1}{QX_2 + QX_1}}{\dfrac{PY_2 - PY_1}{PY_2 + PY_1}}$$

In this formula, QX_2 is the new demand for X, QX_1 is the original demand for X; PY_2 is the new price of Y and PY_1 is the original price of Y.

If X and Y are perfect substitutes for each other, the cross-elasticity of demand will be infinity. It means that the slightest rise in the price of Y will cause an almost infinite rise in the demand for X and the slightest fall in the price of Y will reduce the demand for X to almost zero. If, on the other hand, two goods are no substitutes all, the cross-elasticity of demand will be zero. A change in the price of one commodity will not affect the quantity demanded of the other commodity. It will thus be clear that the cross-elasticity of demand for substitutes varies between zero and infinity.

If the relationship between X and Y is that of complementarily, the cross-elasticity in such a case will be negative. A rise in the price of Y will mean not only a decrease in the quantity demanded of Y but also a decrease in the quantity demanded of X because both are demanded together. For example, ball-point pens and refills are complementary goods. When the price of refills rises, it causes a fall in the demand for refills as well as for ball-point pens, because both are demanded together.

Commodities X and Y will be perfect substitutes only when they are totally identical. In that case, they will not be two different commodities at all. Therefore, in practice, infinite cross-elasticity of demand cannot be found. In practice, the cross-elasticity of a demand can thus be positive, zero or negative. The cross-elasticity is positive when X and Y are good substitutes (and almost infinity when X and Y are almost perfect substitutes). It is zero when X and Y are not related to each other or do not possess any substitutability : they are independent of each other. It is negative when X and Y are complementary goods. In the first case, a rise in the price of Y (price of X remaining constant) will cause an increase in the quantity demanded of X. In the second case, a rise or fall in the price of Y (price of X remaining unchanged) does not affect the quantity demanded of X at all. In the third case, a rise in the price of Y (the price of X remaining unchanged) will cause a decrease in the quantity demanded of X

Example : Because the price of Y increases from Rs. 10 to Rs. 12 per kg., the sales of a firm producing commodity Y rise to 220 kg from 200 kg. per week. Find out the cross-elasticity and state the relationship between commodities X and Y.

$$E_c = \frac{\dfrac{220-200}{220+200}}{\dfrac{12-10}{12+10}} = \frac{\dfrac{20}{420}}{\dfrac{2}{22}}$$

$$= \frac{\dfrac{1}{21}}{\dfrac{1}{11}} = \frac{1}{21} \times \frac{11}{1}$$

$$= 0.52$$

The cross-elasticity of demand is 0.52 and X and Y are substitutes.

Exercise

1) Explain determinants of demand.

2) What is elasticity of demand ? Explain various types of demand elasticity with illustrations.

3) What are the various factors affecting price elasticity of demand?

4) Explain the various methods of measuring Price elasticity of demand

5) Explain types of Income Elasticity of demand.

2.4 CONSUMER BEHAVIOUR

The demand for a commodity depends on the utility of that commodity to a consumer. If a consumer gets more utility from a commodity, he would be willing to pay a higher price and vice- versa.

Meaning of Utility

Utility is the want satisfying power of a commodity. It is a subjective entity and varies from person to person. It should be noted that utility is not the same thing as usefulness. Even harmful things like liquor, may be said to have utility from the economic stand point because people want them. Thus in economics, the concept of utility is ethically neutral.

Utiliiy hypothesis forms the basis for the theory of consumer's behaviour. From time to time different theories have been advanced to explain consumer's behaviour and thus to explain his demand for the product. Two important theories are

(1) Marginal Utility Analysis propounded by Marshall, and

(2) Indifference Curve Analysis.

MARGINAL UTILITY ANALYSIS

This theory which is formulated by Alfred Marshall, a British Economist, seeks to explain how a consumer spends his income on different goods and services so as to attain maximum satisfaction. But before going ito analysis, let us understand the meaning of total utility and marginal utility.

Total utility :

It is the sum of the utility derived from an different units of a commodity consumed by a consumer.

Marginal utility :

It is the additional utility derived from additional unit of a commodity.

Assumptions of Marginal Utility Analysis:

(1) *The Cardinal Measurability of Utility :* According to this theory, utility is a cardinal concept i.e. utility is a measurable and quantifiable entity. Thus a person can say that he derives utility equal to 10 units from the consumption of 1 unit of commodity A and 5 from the consumption of 1 unit of commodity B. Since, he can express his satisfaction quantitatively, he can easily compare different commodities and express which commodity gives better utility or satisfaction and by how much.

According to this theory, money is the measuring rod of utility. The amount of money which a person is prepared to pay for a unit of a good rather than go without it is a measure of the utility which he derives from the good.

(2) *Constancy of the Marginal Utility of Money :* The marginal utility of money remains constant throughout when the individual is spending money on a good. This assumption although not realistic, has been made in order to facilitate the measurement of utility of commodities in terms of money.

(3) *The Hypothesis of Independent Utility :* The total utility which a person gets from the whole collection of goods purchased by him is simply the sum total of the separate utilities of the goods. The theory ignores complementarity between goods.

(4) *Rationality:* Every consumer is rational. He seeks to maximise satisfaction by the maximisation of his total utility subject to the constraint imposed by his given income. How a consumer attains equilibrium position i.e. how he spends his money income on different commodities so as to

derive maximum satisfaction is explained through two important laws:

(i) Law of Diminishing Marginal Utility,

(ii) Law of Equi-Marginal Utility.

(i) The Law of Diminishing Marginal Utility

The law of diminishing marginal utility is based on an important fact that while total wants of a person are virtually unlimited, each single want is satiable.

Since each want is satiable, as *a* consumer consumes more and more units of a good, the intensity of his want for the good goes on decreasing and a point is reached where the consumer no longer wants it.

Marshall who was the exponent of the marginal utility analysis stated the law as follows :

"The additional benefit which a person derives from a given increase in stock of a thing diminishes with every increase in the stock that he already has."

This law describes a very fundamental tendency of human nature. In simple words it says that as a consumer takes more units of a good, the extra satisfaction that he derives from an extra unit of a good goes on falling. It is to be noted that it is the marginal utility and not the total utility which declines with the increase in the consumption of a good.

Table 2.2 : Total and marginal utility schedules

Quantity of coffee consumed (cups per day)	Total utility	Marginal utility
1	30	30
2	50	20
3	65	15
4	75	10
5	83	8
6	89	6
7	93	4
8	96	3
9	98	2
10	99	1
11	95	-4

Let us illustrate the law with the help of an example. Consider Table , in which we have presented the total utility and marginal utility derived by a person from cups of coffee consumed per day. When one cup of coffee is taken per day, the total utility derived by the person is 30 utils (unit of utility) and marginal utility derived is also 30 utils with the consumption of 2nd cup per day the total utility rises to 50 but marginal utility falls to 20.

As the consumption of coffee increases to 10 cups per day, marginal utility from the additional cups goes on diminishing (i.e. the total utility goes on increasing at a diminishing rate). However, when the cups of coffee consumed per day increases to 11, then instead of giving positive marginal utility, the eleventh cup gives negative marginal utility because it may cause him sickness.

when we plot this data, we get the following graph

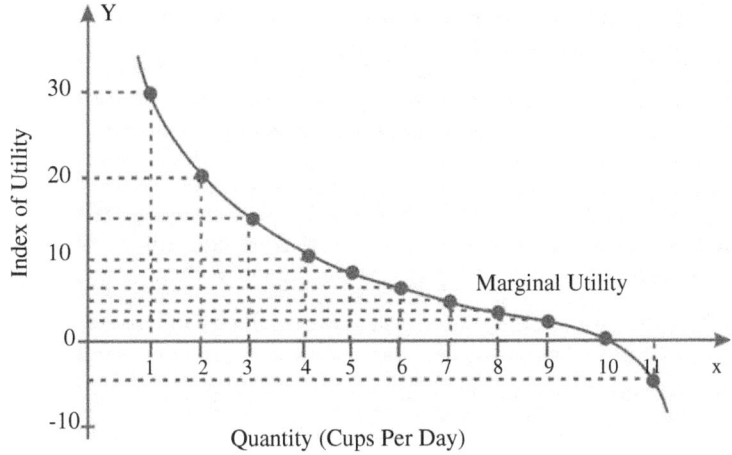

Fig. 2.4 : Marginal utility of coffee consumed

As will be seen from the figure, the marginal utility curve goes on declining throughout. The diminishing marginal utility curve applies almost to all commodities. A few exceptions however, have been pointed out by some economists According to them; this law does not apply to money, music and hobbies. While this may be true in initial stages, beyond a certain limit these will also be subjected to diminishing utility.

Limitations of the Law

The law of diminishing marginal utility is applicable only under certain assumptions.

 (i) The different units consumed should be identical in all respects. The habit, taste, treatment and income of the consumer also remain unchanged.

 (ii) The different units consumed should consist of standard units. If a thirsty man is given water by successive spoonfuls, the utility of second spoonful may conceivably be greater than the utility of the first.

(iii) There should be no time gap or interval between the consumption of one unit and another unit i.e. there should be continuous consumption.

(iv) The law may not apply to articles like gold, cash where a greater quantity may increase the lust for it.

(iv) The shape of the utility curve may be affected by the presence or absence of articles which are substitutes or complements. The utility obtained from coffee may be seriously affected if no sugar is available.

Consumer's Surplus : The concept of consumer's surplus was evolved by Alfred Marshall. This concept occupies an important place not only in economic theory but also in economic policies of government and decision-making of monopolists. Consumers generally are ready to pay more for the goods than they actually pay for them. This extra satisfaction which consumers get from their purchase of goods is called by Marshall as consumer's surplus.Marshall defined the concept of consumer's surplus as "excess of the price which a consumer would be willing to pay rather than go without a thing over that which he actually does pay, is the economic measure of this surplus satisfaction .... it may be called consumer's surplus".

Thus consumer's surplus = What a consumer is ready to pay - What he actually pays.

The concept of consumer's surplus is derived from the law of diminishing marginal utility. As we know from the law of diminishing marginal utility, the more of a thing we have, the lesser marginal utility it has. In other words, as we purchase more of a good, its marginal utility goes on diminishing. The consumer is in equilibrium when marginal utility is equal to given price i.e. he purchases that many number of units of a good at which marginal utility is equal to price (It is assumed that perfect competition prevails in the market). Since the price is fixed for all the units of the good he purchases except for the one at margin, he gets extra utility; this extra utility or extra surplus for the consumer is called consumer's surplus.

Consider following Table in which we have illustrated the measurement of consumer's surplus in case of commodity X

The price of X is assumed to be Rs. 20.

Table 2.3 : Measurement of Consumer's Surplus

No. of units	Marginal Utility	Price (Rs.)	Consumer's Surplus
1	30	20	10
2	28	20	8
3	26	20	6
4	24	20	4
5	22	20	2
6	20	20	0
7	18	20	-

We see from the above table that when consumer's consumption increases from 1 to 2 units, his marginal utility falls from Rs. 30 to Rs. 28. His marginal utility goes on diminishing as he increases his consumption of good X. Since marginal utility for a unit of good indicates the price the consumer is willing to pay for that unit, and since price is assumed to be fixed at Rs. 20, the consumer enjoys a surplus at every unit of purchase above 6 units. Thus when the consumer is purchasing 1 unit of X, the marginal utility is worth Rs. 30 and price fixed is Rs.

20, thus he is deriving a surplus of Rs. 10. Similarly when he purchases 2 units of X, he enjoys a surplus of Rs. 8 [Rs. 28 - Rs. 20]. This continues and he enjoys consumer's surplus equal to Rs. 6, 4, 2 respectively from 3rd, 4th and 5th unit. When he buys 6 units, he is in equilibrium because here his marginal utility is equal to the market price or he is willing to pay a sum equal to the actual market price. Here he enjoys no surplus. Thus, given the price of Rs. 20 per unit, the total surplus which the consumer will get, is Rs. $10 + 8 + 6 + 4 + 2 + 0 = 30$.

The concept of consumer's surplus can also be illustrated graphically. Consider the figure . On the X-axis is measured the amount of the commodity and on the Y-axis the marginal utility and the price of the commodity.

MU is the marginal utility curve which slopes downwards, indicating that as the consumer buys more units of the commodity, its marginal utility falls. Marginal utility shows the price which a person is willing to pay for the different units rather than go without them. If OP is the price that prevails in the market, then consumer will be in equilibrium when he buys OQ units of the commodity, since at OQ units, marginal utility is equal to the given price OP. The last unit, i.e. Qth unit does not yield any consumer's surplus because here price paid is equal to the marginal utility of the Qth unit. But for units before Qth unit, marginal utility is greater than the price and thus these units fetch consumer's surplus to the consumer.

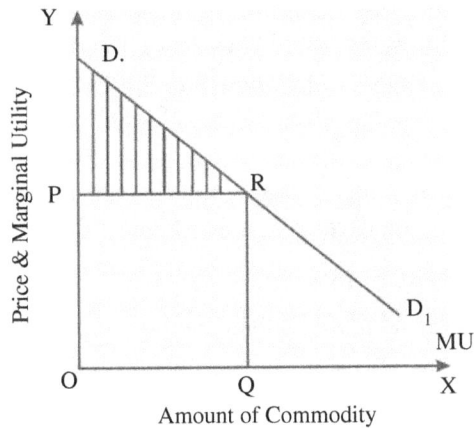

Fig. 2.5 : Marshall's Measure of Consumer's Suplus

In figure the total utility is equal to the area under the marginal utility curve up to point Q i.e. ODRQ. But given the price equal to OP, the consumer actually pays OPRQ. The consumer derives extra utility equal to DPR which is nothing but consumer's surplus.

Usefulness of the Concept

    (i) **Consumer's surplus draws a clear distiction between value-in-use and value-in-exchange** The concept draws attention to the fact that the total utility derived from the consumption of a thing is usually greater than the price paid for it.

   (ii) Consumer's surplus indicates the benefit a person derives from the economic environment in which he lives. We can compare different localities by estimating and comparing the consumer's surplus obtained in each locality. The higher the consumer's surplus, the more advanced is the economy.

(iii) This concept is useful in Public Finance for judging the relative merits of different types of taxation. A tax, generally, raises prices and reduces consumer's surplus. Against the disadvantage can be set off the advantage accruing to the Government in the form of revenue. If the gain to them is less than the loss of consumer surplus, the tax is a bad tax; if the converse obtains, it is a good tax.

(iv) The concept is useful in determining monopoly prices. A monopolist can charge different prices from different consumers according to the consumer surplus earned by them.

Limitations :

(1) Consumer's surplus cannot be measured precisely - because it is difficult to measure the marginal utilities of different units of a commodity consumed by a person.

(2) In the case of necessaries, the marginal utilities of the earlier units are infinitely large. In such case the consumer's surplus is always infinite.

(3) The consumer's surplus derived from a commodity is affected by the availability of substitutes.

(4) There is no simple rule for deriving the utility scale of articles which are used for their prestige value (e.g., diamonds).

(5) Consumer's surplus cannot be measured in terms of money because the marginal utility of money changes as purchases are made and the consumer's stock of money diminishes. (Marshall assumed that the marginal utility of money remains constant. But this assumption is unrealistic).

(6) The concept can be accepted only if it is assumed that utility can be measured in terms of money or otherwise. Many modern economists believe that this cannot be done.

INDIFFERENCE CURVE ANALYSIS

A very popular alternative and more realistic method of explaining consumer's demand is the Indifference Curve Analysis. This approach to consumer behaviour is based on consumer preferences. It believes that human satisfaction being a psychological phenomenon cannot be measured quantitatively in monetary terms as was attempted in Marshall's utility analysis.

Assumptions Underlying Indifference Curve Approach :

(i) The consumer is rational and possesses full information about all the relevant aspects of economic environment in which he lives.

(ii) The consumer is capable of ranking all conceivable combinations of goods according to the satisfaction they yield. Thus if he is given various combinations say A, B, C, D, E he can rank them as first preference, second preference and so on. If a consumer happens to prefer A to B, he cannot tell quantitatively how much he prefers A to B.

(iii) If the consumer prefers combination A to B, and B to C, then he must prefer combination A to C. In other words, he has consistent consumption pattern behaviour.

(iv) If combination A has more commodities than combination B, then A must be preferred to B.

Meaning of Indifference Curves An indifference curve is a curve which represents all those combinations of goods which give same satisfaction to the consumer. Since all the combinations on an indifference curve give equal satisfaction to the consumer, the consumer is indifferent among them. !n other words, since all the combinations provide same level of satisfaction the consumer prefers them equally and does not mind which combination he gets.

To understand indifference curves let us consider the example of a consumer who has one unit of food and 12 units of clothing. Now we ask the consumer how many units of clothing he is prepared to give up to get an additional unit of food, so that his level of satisfaction does not change. Suppose the consumer says that he is ready to give up 6 units of clothing to get an additional unit of food. We will have then two combinations of food and clothing giving equal satisfaction to consumer: Combination A has 1 unit of food and 12 units of clothing, combination B has 2 units of food and 6 units of clothing. Similarly, by asking the consumer further how much of clothing he will be prepared to forgo for successive increments in his stock of food so that his level of satisfaction remains unaltered, we get various combinations as given below:

Table 2.4 : Indifference Schedule

Combination	Food	Clothing
A	1	12
B	2	6
C	3	4
D.	4	3

Now if we draw the above schedule we will get the following figure.

In the figure, an indifference curve 1C is drawn by plotting the various combinations of the indifference schedule. The quantity of food is measured on the X axis and the quantity of clothing on the Y axis. As in indifference schedule, combinations lying on an indifference curve will give the consumer same level of satisfaction.

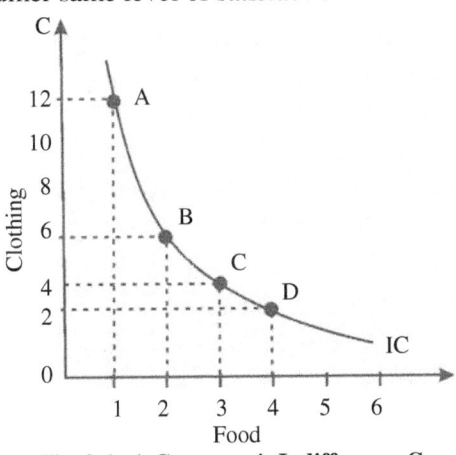

Fig. 2.6 : A Consumer's Indifference Curve

Indifference Map :

A set of indifference curves is called indifference map,

An indifference map depicts complete picture of consumer's tastes and preferences, in the following figure an indifference map of a consumer is shown which consists of three indifference curves.

We have taken good X on X-axis and good Y on Y-axis. It should be noted that while the consumer is indifferent among the combinations lying on the same indifference curve, he certainly prefers the combinations on the higher indifference curve to the combinations lying on a lower indifference curve because a higher indifference curve signifies a higher level of satisfaction. Thus while all combinations of IC_1. give same satisfaction, all combinations lying on IC_2 give greater satisfaction than those lying on IC_1.

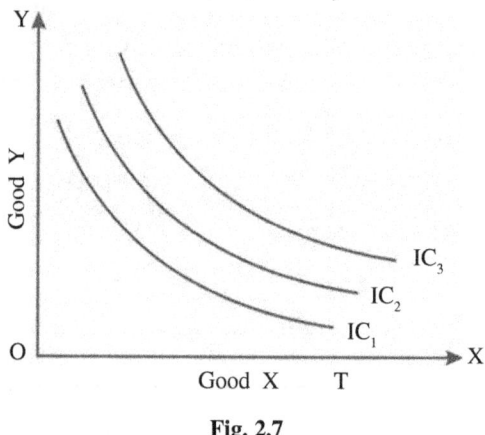

Fig. 2.7

Properties of Indifference Curves :

The following are the main characteristics or properties of indifference curves:

(i) Indifference curves slope downward to the right: This property implies that when the amount of one good in combination is increased, the amount of the other good is reduced. This is essential if the level of satisfaction is to remain the same on an indifference curve.

(ii) Indifference curves are always convex to the origin: It has been observed that as more and more of one commodity (X) is substituted for another (Y), the consumer is willing to part with less and less of the commodity being substituted (i.e. Y). This is called diminishing marginal rate of substitution. Thus in our example of food and clothing, as a consumer has more and more units of food, he is prepared to forego less and less units of clothing. This happens mainly because want for a particular good is satiable and as a person has more and more of a good, his intensity of want for that good goes on diminishing. This diminishing marginal rate of substitution gives convex shape to the indifference curves.

(iii) Indifference curves can never intersect each other : No two indifference curves will intersect each other although it is not necessary that they are parallel to each other. In case of intersection the relationship becomes logically absurd because it would show that higher and lower levels are equal which is not possible. This property will be clear from the following figure

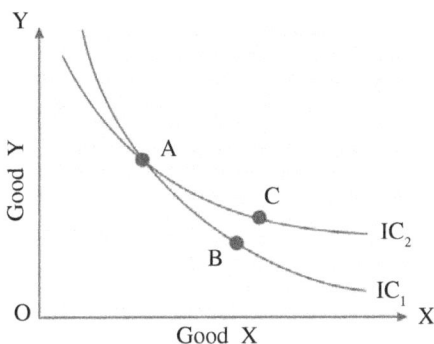

Fig. 2.8 : Intersecting Indifference Curves

In the figure IC_1, and $1C_2$, intersect at A. Since A and B lies on IC_1 they give same satisfaction to the consumer. Similarly since A and C lie on IC_2, they give same satisfaction to the consumer. This implies that combination B and C are equal in terms of satisfaction. But this is an absurd conclusion because certainly combination C is better than combination B because it contains more units of commodities X and Y. Thus we see that no two indifference curves can touch or cut each other,

(iv) *A higher indifference curve represents a higher level of satisfaction than the lower indifference curve :* This is because combinations lying en a higher indifference curve contain more of either one for both goods and more goods are preferred to less of them.

Budget Line :

A higher indifference curve shows a higher level of satisfaction than a lower one. Therefore, a consumer in his attempt to maximise satisfaction will try to reach the highest possible indifference curve. But in his pursuit of buying more and more goods and thus obtaining more and more satisfaction he has to work under two constraints: firstly, he has to pay the prices for the goods and, secondly, he has a limited money income with which to purchase the goods.

These constraints are explained by budget line or price line. In simple words a budget line shows all those combinations of two goods which the consumer can buy spending his given money income on the two goods at their given prices. All those combinations which are within the reach of the consumer assuming that he spends all his money income will lie on the budget line.

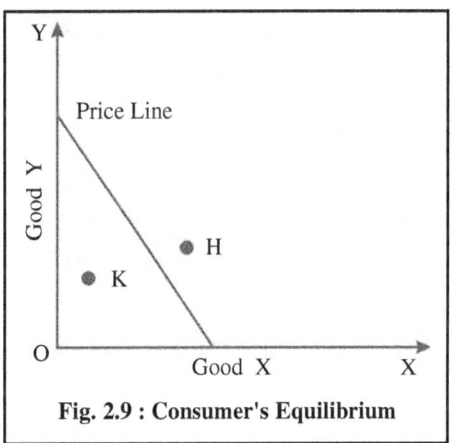

Fig. 2.9 : Consumer's Equilibrium

It should be noted that any point outside the given price line, like H, will be beyond the reach of the consumer and any combination lying within the line, like K, shows under spending by the consumer.

Consumer's Equilibrium :

A consumer is in equilibrium when he is deriving maximum possible satisfaction from the goods and is in no position to rearrange his purchases ot goods. We assume that:

(i) the consumer has a given indifference map which shows his scale of preferences for various combinations of two goods X and Y.

(ii) he has a fixed money income which he has to spend wholly on goods X and Y.

(iii) prices of goods X and Y are given and are fixed for him.

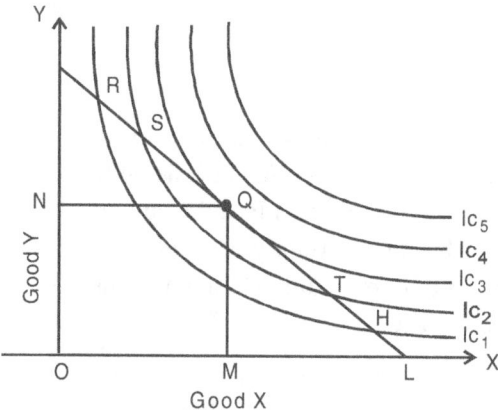

Fig. 2.10 : Consumer's Equilibrium

To show which combination of two goods X and Y the consumer will buy to be in equilibrium we bring his indifference map and budget line together.

The indifference map depicts the consumer's preference scale between various combinations of two goods and the budget line shows various combinations which he can afford to buy with his given money income and prices of the two goods. Consider the above figure 2.10 in which IC_1, IC_2, IC_3, IC_4 and IC_5 are shown together with budget line PL for good X and good Y. Every combination on budget line PL costs the same. Thus combinations R, S, Q, T and H cost the same to the consumer. The consumer's aim is to maximise his satisfaction and for this he will try to reach highest indifference curve.

But since there is a budget constraint he will be forced to remain on the given budget line, that is he will have to choose any combinations from among only those which lie on the given price line.

If he chooses R, but we see that R lies on *a* lower indifference curve IC_1, when he can very well afford S, Q or T lying on higher indifference curve. Similar is the case for other combinations on IC_1, like H. Again, suppose he chooses combination S (or T) lying on IC_2. But here again we see that the consumer can still reach a higher level of satisfaction remaining within his budget constraints i.e. he can afford to have combination Q lying on IC_3 because it lies on his budget line. Now what if he chooses combination Q? We find that this is the best choice because this combination lies not only on his budget line but also puts him on highest possible indifference curve i.e. IC_3. The consumer can very well wish to reach IC_4 or IC_5, but these indifference curves are beyond his reach given his money income. Thus the consumer will be at equilibrium at point Q on IC_3. What do we notice at point Q? We notice that at this point, his budget line PL is tangent to the indifference curve IC_3. In this equilibrium position (at Q), the consumer will buy OM of X and ON of Y.

At the tangency point Q, the slopes of the price line PL and indifference curve IC_3 are equal. The slope of the indifference curve shows the marginal rate of substitution of X for Y (MRSxy) which is equal to $\dfrac{MU_x}{MU_y}$ while the slope of the price line indicates the ratio between the prices of two goods Px / Py.

At equilibrium point Q,

$$MRSxy = \frac{MU_x}{MU_y} = \frac{P_x}{P_y}$$

Therefore the condition for the equilibrium can be expressed in either of the two ways : Price line must be tangent to the indifference curve or the marginal rate of substitution of goods X and Y must be equal to the ratio between the prices of the two goods.

Exercise

1) Explain the law of diminishing marginal utility giving examples.
2) Giving main assumptions show how a consumer is in equilibrium under marginal utility analysis.
3) What are indifference curves? How does a consumer reach equilibrium under the indifference curve analysis?
4) What is consumer's surplus? How is it measured? What are the various uses and limitations of the concept of consumer's surplus.

2.5 Demand Estimation and Demand Forecasting

Demand Estimation (Short Period) :

Knowing the demand for its product is a significant activity for the firm. The existing firm must know what will be the current demand, say over a month and a half or a year for its product so that it can avoid overproduction or underproduction. Such information will enable the firm not only to avoid overproduction or underproduction, but also to determine its price policy, promotional policy etc. Then only it can secure optimum sales, or optimal revenue or maximum profit. Such information about the **current demand for a firm product is called Demand estimation.** Here demand data is collected for a short period, usually a year or less.

Demand estimation may be defined as the process of finding current values of demand for various values of prices and other determining variables. **Demand estimation for the firm's product is for a short period.**

Demand Forecasting (Long Period) :

Demand Forecasting :

The firm may not be much interested in short term demand estimation. It may be interested in production planning, new product development, investment for expansion in new schemes, etc. It may desire to plan for long-term financial investment and for long-term manpower requirements. Here, the decisions have effects over a long period of time. It takes time for a firm to be erected. The actual production starts after a considerable periods of time, say, two years, five years or in some cases even ten years, e.g. large steel plants require ten to fifteen years for construction. It is, therefore necessary to forecast demand five years hence, ten years hence and so on. This is called demand forecasting. Demand forecasting may be defined as the process of finding values for demand in the future time periods. Demand forecasting is for a long period. The other name is business forecasting.

Objectives of Demand Estimation (Short Period) :

Demand estimation has the following objectives:

1. To reduce costs of raw materials and control inventories; to stock enough raw materials according to demand estimates.
2. To arrange for short term financial requirements, such as working capital for day to day requirements.
3. To set sales targets based on demand estimation and to provide incentives to sales people.
4. To arrange for appropriate promotional efforts such as advertising and sales campaigns etc.
5. To prepare proper price policies for achieving essential results. If the demand estimation is bright, too low prices will be damaging and if the demand conditions are duly maintaining a higher price level will be damaging to the interests of the firm.
6. To plan production programs so that there is neither overproduction nor underproduction. Production programmes should be in line with the expected sales as per the demand estimation.

Objectives of Demand Forecasting (Long Period) :

Demand forecasting, which is for a long period , has the following objectives:

1. Long period demand forecasting is necessary for ascertaining future demand for the product so that the firm can plan new units, new projects, new plants, expansion of existing scale operation. Knowledge of growth trends in economy related to income and other variables is essential. Their likely impact on the aggregate demand and the demand for the firm's products can be ascertained. In the case of the firms producing inputs or intermediate products, demand forecasting of the consumers' final product in the production of which inputs are used, is very much essential. It can find out the probable increase or decrease in the demand of such inputs.
2. Demand forecasting will be advantageous for finding out the lines of profitable investments before taking the risk of new investments, particularly for large firms.
3. Demand forecasting is also necessary to prepare plans for long-term financial requirements. Then only can the firm proceed to arrange for the same through equity and debenture issues and long-term loans.

4. Long term sales forecasts help the firm in planning for trained manpower. It can start training schemes well in time for future expansion programmes and also for adapting itself to new products likely to come up in the market.

5. Long term demand forecasting also helps in developing different processes and departments under the same roof, if there is going to be a heavy growth in the demand for the product.

Even though we have used the term demand estimation to find out the current values of output of the product demanded in the short period, and the term demand forecasting to find out the values of output of the product in the long period, in most textbooks, the term Demand Forecasting is used generally for both short term and long term forecasting. To distinguish between the estimation of current values and forecasting of future values, the terms Short-Term Forecasting and Long-Term Forecasting may be used respectively.

Direct and Indirect Methods of Demand Estimation :
Direct Methods :

The following are the direct methods of demand estimation (short period) :
I. Consumer's surveys
II. Expert's opinion
III. Simulated market situation
IV. Controlled market experiments

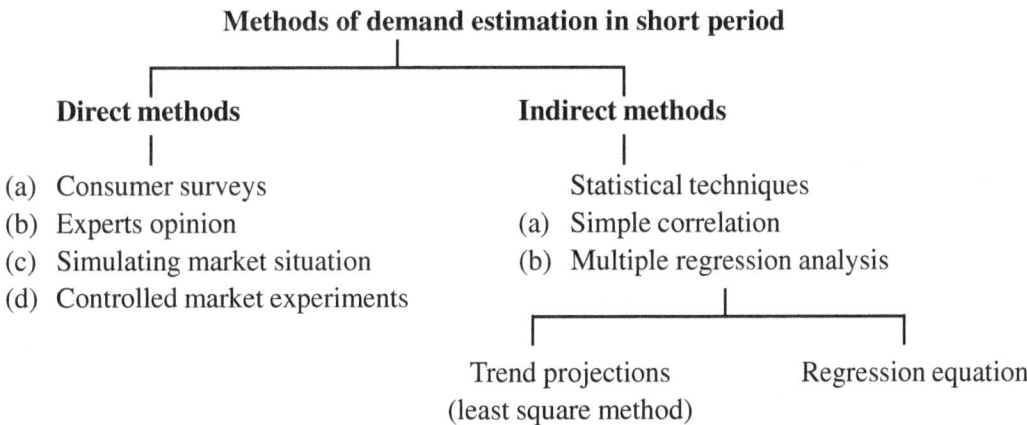

Methods of demand estimation in short period

Direct methods
(a) Consumer surveys
(b) Experts opinion
(c) Simulating market situation
(d) Controlled market experiments

Indirect methods
Statistical techniques
(a) Simple correlation
(b) Multiple regression analysis

Trend projections (least square method)   Regression equation

Indirect Methods :

Statistical techniques are used in indirect methods. On the basis of past data, statistical relationship between the dependent and the independent variables are found out. The statistical tools of simple correlation and multiple regression analysis are used to find out these relationships.

Direct Methods :

1. Consumers' Surveys :

Intentions of buyers or potential buyers are recorded through **personal interviews, mail or post surveys and telephone interviews.**

Questionnaires are prepared to find out buyers' intentions. For example, with regard to their reaction to a price change or a change in some other variable, such as advertising, quality, packing etc. The work of consumers' surveys should be given to trained, reliable and experienced professionals. Questionnaires should not be very complicated.

In **personal interview method,** house to house survey is made. One advantage of the personal interview is that the interviewer can explain questions to the person who may not understand them. But this method is **expensive and time consuming.**

In case **of post or mail surveys,** the cost is much less and it covers a large area in a short period. However since there is no personal meeting, explanation of questions is not possible and therefore there is a possibility of receiving useless answers.

Telephone Interviews have an advantage of personal touch and are time and money saving. However, in less developed countries, telephone services are not available to all customers. Besides, long interviews cannot be conducted over telephones. Telephone surveys are preferable only when quick information from consumers is desired, that too, on one or two matters related to the product.

Limitations Consumer Surveys :

1. Since the buyer is asked hypothetical questions, his answers are also hypothetical.
2. The answers may not reveal the buyers true intentions.
3. The buyer may feel that the interviewer wants a particular kind of response.
4. Instead of revealing his intentions he may reply what he feels is expected and may reply to please the interviewer.
5. Even if the buyer reveals his true intentions he may me:change his decision while making his actual purchases.

Types of Consumer Surveys :

There are two types of consumer surveys :
1. Complete Enumeration Method
2. Sample Survey Method

1. Complete Enumeration Method :

In the complete enumeration method all potential buyers of the product are contacted. The survey covers all the potential consumers in the market and ther interviews are conducted to find out the probable demand. Once individual demands for the product are ascertained by the complete "enumeration method, these are added together to find the total demand for the firm's product.

Advantages of Complete Enumeration Method :

1. Since all potential consumers are contacted, there is a greater deal of **accuracy** in this method. This depends on whether the consumers have expressed their true opinions or not.

2. This method is more useful when new products are to be introduced into the market.

3. This method may prove beneficial for products for which the number of potential consumers is small. E.g. for bulky and costly products like cars, machines and refrigerators.

Disadvantages of Complete Enumeration Method :

1. This method is expensive as the survey covers the entire fleet of enumerators.

2. It is time consuming. A great deal of time is consumed, since all consumers are interviewed.

3. The method is ,of no use where the consumers are spread over a wide area and cannot be contacted easily.

4. In the absence of a large number of qualified and competent investigators this method will not work effectively and is less reliable.

2. Sample Survey Method : Due to the limitations of the complete enumeration method, sample surveys are more popular for demand estimation. In this method only a few consumers selected from the total potential consumers are interviewed and then the average demand is calculated on the basis of consumers interviewed. By multiplying the total of consumers by this average demand, the aggregate demand for this product is estimated.

Methods of Sample surveys :

There are two types of Sample surveys

1. Random or Probability Sampling

2. Non-Random ,or non-probability Sampling Random Sampling :

Random Sampling :

In the case of probability or random surveys, the law of probability can be applied. In this method each consumer or group of consumers is given an equal chance of being selected for the sampling. Selection is made with the help of a table of random numbers. There are five random sampling methods:

- Simple Random Sampling
- Stratified Sampling
- Systematic Sampling
- Cluster Sampling
- Multi- Phase-Samplifig

Non Random Sampling :

For certain purposes non random sampling method is used. There are three important types of non-random or non- probability samples.

- Judgment Sampling
- Quota Sampling
- Convenience Sampling

1. **Judgment Sampling :** The investigator uses his discretion or judgement in choosing sample items. He prefers those items for samples which according to his judgement, are most representative of the universe.

2. **Quota Sampling :** Where quotas are allocated for the purpose of judgement sampling, it is known as quota sampling. The investigator is asked to choose the items of the sample according to quotas for different categories for the items.

3. **Convenience Sampling :** It is also known as chunk sampling. In this type, a chunk or a fraction of the universe is chosen for the investigation of the survey on the basis of convenience. The sample or the chunk is selected by convenience, e.g. the sample may be readily available from a printed list, e.g. the list of telephone subscribers from a telephone directory, or from the list of members from various clubs, institutions, etc. Interviews may be conducted at bus stops, railway stations, or busy market roads to find out the responses for the product. Since convenience sampling cannot be representatives of the universe, its results are not satisfactory or reliable.

Merits of Sampling Techniques :

1. **Less costly :** Only a small number of consumers are interviewed and hence the total cost of the survey tends to be small.

2. **Less Time Consuming :** Time is saved in both collecting data and processing it.

3. **More Reliable :** The extent of sampling error can be determined. This is because greater precautions can be taken when a small number of consumers are interviewed. Follow up work is easier and is more effectively done in the case of sampling method.

4. **More Information Obtained with Less Cost and Time :** Under sampling survey method, detailed information is obtained without any increase in the expenses. The collection of information can be better organized with the help of investigators, whose number would be much less in the case of complete enumeration method. Therefore there is more concentration, more care and more diligence while obtaining information.

Limitations of Sampling Survey :

1. **Necessity of qualified and expert investigators :** Sample survey results depend much on the competence of the field investigators and experts.

2. **Careful planning** necessary

3. **Chances of errors :** Unless sample size is reasonably high, the chances of errors increase.

III) Expert Opinion Survey:

It is also known as sales force polling. There are certain categories of people who are in the know of the market. They know the consumers responses to the products. These are salesmen, market consultants and professional experts. These people deal in the products or have studied market trends and consumer behavior for years; they know the future plans of the consumersw, their reactions to the new products, demand for rival products, etc.

A firm having a **large band of salesmen** in various regions, may ask them to **undertake surveys** in their regions regarding the expected future demand for product and to collect allied information such as their responses to advertising quality changes, price change, etc. The data thus collected may be consolidated, tabulated, and inferences about the demand in the short term period are drawn. Then taking into consideration the changes in the other variables, such as income of the consumer, income distribution, population, employments and effects of promotional efforts, advertising campaigns, exhibition displays, door to door canvassing of the products, etc., degree of competition form rival-firms, the firm comes to the final sales estimation of the product.

Aid of marketing managers, managerial economists, production managers, sales managers and other top executives may be taken to conduct expert opinion surveys. This method is also called "collective opinion" methodbecause its forecasts are based on the aggregate opinion of the experts in the field. It is also caIIved "Hunch" method, as it; gjves forecasting bjised on the hunches of the experts.

Advantages of 'Experts' Opinion Surveys :

1. This method is **simple and less costly.**
2. It enables the firm to estimate current demand in the short period, very quickly. This method is thus more **time saving.**
3. This method is useful for **new products** introduced in the market, where no data is available.
4. Since the opinions about sales estimation come from experts, they are likely to be **more reliable.**
5. The firm gets different points of view which are then **balanced** in the process.

Limitations of Experts' Opinion Survey :

1. Opinions of the firm's own sales representative may be **biased.**
2. These opinions are **subjective and may not be fully reliable,** unless the salesmen are well experienced.
3. While expressing their opinions about the sales in the short term period, the salesmen **may not consider the effect of changes** in other independent variables such as income, advertising, etc.

(IV) Simulated Market Situation :

An **artificial market situation** is created and the participants are Selected. These are called called consumer clinics. Selected participantsare given a ciejtainjsum of money and are asked to spend it on an artificial departmental store. The reponses of the participants to price changes of varied amounts and to different promotional efforts are observed. Accordingly necessary decisions about price changes are taken.

Such a kind of simulated market situation may have many **limitations:**

1. This method is **time consuming**
2. Selection of participants is again a **difficult job.**
3. Participants in order to show that they are thrifty may **buy cheap products only**
4. When a person buys with someone else's money he **may behave differently** as compared to when he buys with his own money.
5. Such consumer clinics are an **expensive method** of obtaining data.
6. Lastly the results obtained **may not be fully representative** of the consumer market.

(V) Controlled Market Experiments :

A firm may conduct the same simulated market situation experiment as described abpve in an **actual market.**

A firm may reduce the price in the actual market and **observe buyers reactions** and compare the sales resulting from the price reduction with the sales in the past. It may fix up different prices in different markets and **observe the responses of the buyers.** It first finds out the buyers responses. If. the responses are good then the firm may take the risk of spending huge amounts of money on such compaigns on a nationwide basis.

Precautions to be taken : **Firstly,** While selecting markets for controlled experiments, **areas** selected should have **the same characteristics** such as income levels, population, social background, tastes and preferences, occupational pattern, etc.

Secondly such experiments should be conducted over **an extended period of time** to observe more than just initial or impact effects of price change or some other variable such as advertising, packaging, quality etc. To know whether the changes are due to uncontrollable factors such as increase or decrease in income levels, changes in income distribution, changes in fashion, etc., "controlled market experiments" may be conducted and effects of such uncontrollable factors may be separated in order to know the net effect of controllable variables.

Benefits of Controlled Market Experiments :

1. The major benefit of controlled market experiments is that the firm knows the actual responses of the buyers to variation in controlled factors such as price of the product, sales promotion campaigns etc. Instead of spending a large amount on nationwide campaigns, it can conduct a test by introducing its new campaign in smaller areas to find out the buyers reactions.
2. If the experiments are carefully performed the firm is saved from the dangers of underpricing, overpricing or unnecessary spending of money on wasteful advertisements.

Limitations of Controlled Market Experiments :

1. It may happen that changes in sales in the controlled market may not be due to variations in the controlled variables. They may be a result of changes in the uncontrollable factors. Effect of uncontrollable factors should be separated in order to get the net effect of the controllable factors. Otherwise the results would be misleading.

2. If the experiment is conducted over a very short period the **results may not be reliable.**

3. Market experiments become an **expensive exercise.**

4. If the promotion campaign fails in its experiment it may **do long term damage** to the firm's image and to its sales level.

5. While the firm introduces a price change or a change in the promotional efforts like new advertising campaign in its market experiment, it is quite likely that the **rival firms may nullify** such an experiment" and the entire effort of the firm to conduct such an experiment may go wasted.

Indirect Methods :

Indirect methods of demand estimation consist of simple correlation (Regression Analysis) and Trend Projections

I. Simple Correlation (Regression Analysis) :.

Regression analysis is the most popular method of demand estimation. This method **combines ecomomic theory and statistical techniques of estimation. Economic theory** is employed to specify the determinants of demand and to determine the nature of the relationship between the demand for a product and its determinants i.e. in determining **the general form of demand function. Statistical techniques** are employed to estimate the **values of parameters** in the estimated equation. It is a very useful technique to find out the change in the quantities of the product demanded, when other independent variables such as price, income, tastes, advertising etc., change., Suppose, two variables X (say advertising* expenditure) and Y (sales) are closely related, we can find out with the help of regression equation the probable value of Y (sales) for a given value of X (advertising expenditure). For economists, producers and business people, the study of regression is of immense help.

When we consider the. relationship between two variables - one dependent variable (eg. Sales) and another independent variable (eg. Price) , the relationship is called **Simple Regression or simple correlation.** Where the relationship is between the dependent variable and a number of independent variables, it is known as **Multiple Regression.** Solving regression equations and finding out the values is very complex and requires time. However, with the aid of computer programmes, simple and multiple regressions can be estimated quickly and easily. Since regression analysis is a complex statistical technique, it forms a study by itself.

Limitations in Regression Analysis :

1. Even though the regression analysis is of vital help in demand estimation and demand forecasting?, it is not 100 per cent reliable.

2. The result may be spurious, and, therefore, giving misleading explanation and poor forecasting.

3. There may be the omission of important independent variables. This may lead to probable unreliability in the regression coefficient.

4. There is a pitfall of the improper measurement of the variables. For example, the price

variable may be taken from the 'list price' or 'manufacturer's suggested price', but in actual reality, customer bargaining, discounts etc., may be involved and the actual payments may be less than the list price.

II. Trend Projections :

In this method, past data about the dependent variable and other independent variables is used to project the sales in the coming year or years. This method is called **Time Series Analysis Method.** Here, the pairs of observations recorded over time in a particular situation is used. For example, data about the sales of the product in the past five years is collected. The resulting trend is then extrapolated into future periods. The result and indicated sales levels are used as the basis for the demand estimation.

Methods of Demand Forecasting :

There are several methods and techniques available for forecasting demand for a product. All the methods have-their own limitations and advantages, merits and demerits, in varying degrees. The applicability and usefulness of a method depends on a purpose of forecasting and availability of reliable and relevant data. The analyst should, therefore, choose a method or a technique of demand forecasting which is relevant to the purpose, convenient to handle, applicable to the available data and also inexpensive.

I. Trend Projection or Trend Extrapolation :

This is a statistical technique by which the established relationship from the past data is projected into the future. However in this method new information obtained from consumers' and investors' surveys cannot be incorporated to modify the established relationships. This method is essentially concerned with the study of movement of variables through time. The use of this method requires a long and reliable time series data. The trend projection method is used under the assumption that the factors responsible for the past trends in the variable to be projected(for e.g. sales and demand) will continue to play their part in future in the same manner and to the same extent as they did in the past in determining the magnitude and direction of the variable.

In projecting demand for a product the trend method is applied to time series data on sales. Firms of a long standing may obtain time series data on sales from their own sales department. New firms can obtain necessary data from the older firms belonging to the same industry.

Merits of Trend Projection :

1. This method is quite popular in business forecasting because of its simplicity. It is simple to apply because only time series data on sales are required.
2. The analyst is suppose to possess only a working knowledge of statistics.
3. Since data requirement of this method is limited, it is also inexpensive.
4. The trend method yields fairly reliable estimates of the future course of demand.

Limitations of Trend Projection :

1. Although this method is very simple and least expensive, the projections made through this method are not very reliable. The reason is that the extension of the trend line involves subjectivity and personal bias of the analyst.
2. This method cannot be used for short term estimates.
3. It does not yield necessary information which can be used ofr future policy formulations.

II. Leading Indicators:

This is a barometric indicator. The barometric method of forecasting follows the method that meteorologists use on weather forecastion. Meteorologists use the barometer to forecastnweather conditions on the basis of movements of mercury in the barometer. Follqwing the logic of this method many economists use **economic indicators** as a barometer to forecast trends in business activities. This method has been developed to forecast the **general trend** in overall economic activities. Nevertheless this method can be used to **forecast demand prospects** for a product, not the actual quantity expected to be demanded.

The **leading indicators** consist of a **leading series** which move up or down Imead of some other series. Some examples of leading indicators are:

1. Bank rate
2. Index of net business (capital) formation.
3. New orders for durable goods.
4. New building permits.
5. Change in the value of inventories.
6. Index of prices of materials.
7. Corporate profits after tax
8. Change in consumer debt.

Limitations :

1. Barometric indicators predict **turning points** only.
2. The **extent of change** cannot be measured.
3. Can be used only for **short term forecasting.**
4. The leading series indices may lead **in different directions.**

Conclusion :

Thus, forecasting is merely an attempt to utilize the generally accepted methods or techniques for knowing the future demand for a product. By the very nature of the problem, there can be no guarantee of accuracy in any specified methodology or system of indicators. There is need for continual revision so that forecast gets closer to reality.

Exercise

1. Explain methods of demand forecasting.
2. What is demand estimations? Explain methods of demand estimation.
3. What are the objectives of Demand Estimation?
4. What are the objectives of demand forecasting?

Production and Cost Analysis

Contents

3.1 MEANING OF PRODUCTION

Production is a very important economic activity. The standard of living of people depends on the volume and variety of production. In fact, the performance of an economy is judged by the level of its production. Those countries which produce goods in large quantities are rich and those which produce less are poor. Thus, the amount of goods and services an economy is able to produce determines the 'richness or poverty of that economy. The U.S.A. is a rich country just because its level of production is high while India is not so rich because its level of production is not very high.

In common parlance the term 'Production' is used for an activity of making something material. But in economics the word 'production' is used in a wider sense. In economics, by production we mean the process by which man utilises or converts the resources of nature, working upon them so as to make them satisfy human wants. Whether it is the making of material goods or providing any service, it is included in production provided it satisfies the wants of some people. So, in economics, if making of cloth by an industrial worker is production, the work of doctors, lawyers, teachers, actors, dancers etc. is also production since the services are provided by them to satisfy the wants of those who pay for them. The satisfying power of goods and services is called utility. Hence, Production means creation or addition of utility.

Utility can be created in the following ways

    (i) *Form utility :* Changing the form of natural resources. Most manufacturing processes consist of taking raw material and transforming them into some items possessing utility, e.g., changing the form of a log of wood into a table or changing the form of iron into a machine.

    (ii) *Place utility :* Changing the place of the resources, from the place where they are of little or no use to another place where they are of greater use. For example, removal of coal, minerals, gold and other metal ores from mines and supplying them to markets.

    (iii) *Time utility :* Storage or Preservation creates time utility.Making available materials at times when they are not normally available e.g., harvested food grains are stored for use till next harvest. Canning of seasonal fruits is undertaken to make them available during off season.

    (iv) *Possession utility :* Utility is also created when a commodity is possessed by a person who can derive satisfaction out of it.

    (v) *Service utility :* Service provided also has utility. The services of doctors, lawyers, teachers, actors, dancers etc provide service utility.

    (vi) *Knowledge utility :* Utility can be created through spread of knowledge.

3.2 PRODUCTION FUNCTION :

Production function states the relationship between inputs and output i.e., the maximum amount of output that can be produced with given quantities of inputs under a given state of technical knowledge. The output takes the form of volume of goods or services and the inputs are the different factors of production i.e., land, labour, capital and enterprise. Mathematically, the production function is described as:

$$p = f(x_1, x_2, x_3 \dots x_{11})$$

Where p is the quantity produced during a given period of time and $(x_1, x_2, x_3 \dots x_{11})$ are the quantities of various inputs used in production.

Production function can also be defined in a different way. It shows the minimum quantities of various inputs that are required to yield a given quantity of output.

The production function of a firm can be studied in the context of short period or long period. Short-period or short-run is that period of time which is too short for a firm to install a new capital equipment to increase production. It implies capital is a fixed factor in the short run and the production function is studied by holding the quantities of capital fixed, while varying the amount of other factors (labour, raw material etc.). This is done when the law of variable proportion is derived. The production function can also be studied in the long-run. The long run is a period of time in which all the factors of production are variable. It is a time period when the firm will be able to install new machines and capital equipments apart from increasing the units of labour. The behaviour of production when all factors are varied is the subject matter of the laws of returns to scale.

Cobb-Douglas Production Function :

One of the famous empirically analysed production functions is the Cobb-Douglas Production Function which in its original form is applied to the whole of the manufacturing industry. In this function, there are two inputs, labour and capital. The mathematical form of the Cobb-Douglas production function is

$$Q = K.L^a \ C^b$$

Where Q is the output, L is the quantity of labour. C is the quantity of capital and 'K' is a positive constant and 'a' and 'b' denote the elasticity of output with respect to labour and capital respectively.

The Cobb-Douglas production function exhibits constant returns to scale. It says that about 75 per cent of the increase in production is due to labour and 25 per cent is due to capital.

3.3 LAW OF VARIABLE PROPORTIONS OR LAW OF DIMINISHING RETURNS:

The law of variable proportions or the law of diminishing returns examines the production function with one factor variable, keeping quantities of other factors fixed. In other words, it refers to input-output relationship, when the output is increased by varying the quantity of one input. This law operates in the short run 'when all the factors of production cannot be increased or decreased simultaneously (for example, we cannot build a plant or. dismantle a plant in the short run). The law operates under certain assumptions which are as follows:

1. The state of technology is assumed to be given and unchanged. If there is any improvement in technology, then marginal and average product may rise instead of falling.
2. There must be some inputs whose quantity is kept fixed. This law does not apply to cases when all factors are proportionately varied. When all the factors are proportionately varied, laws of returns to scale are applicable.
3. The law does not apply to those cases where the factors must be used in fixed proportions to yield product. When the various factors are required to be used in fixed proportions, then an increase in one factor would not lead to any increase in output i.e., marginal product of the variable factor will then be zero and not diminishing.
4. We consider only physical inputs and outputs and not economic profitability in monetary terms.

The law states that as we increase the quantity of one input which is combined with other fixed inputs, the marginal physical productivity of the variable input must eventually decline. In other words, an increase in some inputs relative to other fixed inputs will, in a given state of technology, cause output to increase; but after a point the extra output resulting from the same addition of extra inputs will become less and less.

The behaviour of output when the varying quantity of one factor is combined with a fixed quantity of the others can be divided into three distinct stages or laws.

Before discussing the law, it would be appropriate to understand the meaning of total product, average product and marginal product.

Total Product (TP): Total product is the total output resulting from the efforts of all the factors of production combined together at any time. If the inputs of all but one factor are held constant, total product will vary with the quantity used of the variable factor.

Average Product (AP): Average product is the total product per unit of the variable factor.

Marginal Product (MP): Marginal product is the change in total product per unit change in the quantity of variable factor. In other words, it is the addition made to the total production by an additional unit of input.

The law of variable proportions can be explained with the following illustration

Suppose a farmer has 3 hectares of land and a given amount of capital in terms of a well a set of implements etc. By keeping land and capital constant, the farmer goes on increasing the number of workers. With one variable factor (labour) combined with two fixed factors, the output, say, changes as shown in table 3.1 below.

The table clearly shows that the extra output or increments in total product i.e. marginal product at first increases but after a certain point, starts declining, as the variable input labour is increased by equal amounts. See the last column, i.e. the column of marginal product, in the table. Marginal product increases from 10 to 14 when the number of workers is increased from 1 to 3. But after that, as the number of workers is further increased, one by one, the marginal product goes on declining still further.

Table 3.1 Effect of One Variable factor on Production

Number of Workers	Total Product (Quintals)	Average Product (Quintals)	Marginal Product (Quintals)
1	10	10	10
2	22	11	12
3	36	12	14
4	48	12	12
5	55	11	7
6	60	10	5
7	63	9	3
8	63	7.8	0
9	54	6	-9

Average-Marginal Relations

Table 3.1 shows that eventually total product also starts declining. But, first to decline is the marginal product. The relationship between average and marginal product is a typical or and can be discovered from the table.

1. So long as the marginal product exceeds average product (see columns 3 and 4), each new average product will be larger than the previous one. In other words, average output continues to increase. Conversely, as long as average output is rising, marginal output or marginal product would be larger than average product.

2. Average product begins to decline when the marginal product goes below the average product. In other words, marginal product is less than the average product when the average product is decreasing.

3. The average product remains constant, when the marginal and average products are equal. Also, when the average product is maximum, marginal product equals averag product.

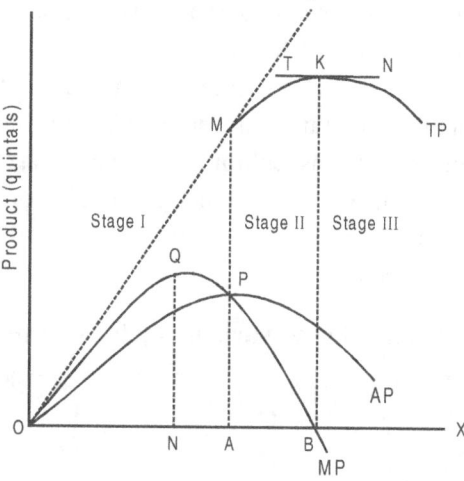

Variable factor (no. of workers)

Fig. 3.1 : Law of Variable Proportions

4. Total product is maximum when marginal product is zero. The Law of Variable Proportions can be illustrated diagrammatically, as shown in Fig. 3.1. Curve TP is the total product curve. With increase in variable factor (number of workers), the total product goes on increasing. Average and marginal products also increase. So long as both marginal and average products are increasing, marginal product curve (MP) lies above average product curve. The marginal product curve cuts the average product curve from above at point P where the average product (AP) is the maximum and the average and marginal products are equal. Once the average product curve (AP) starts sloping downwards, the MP curve lies below the AP curve. In fact, as we can see from the table, the average product falls because the marginal product is falling. At point B, the MP curve cuts the X-axis, means that at point B the marginal product is zero. At this point, the total product is the maximum (BK). Thus total product is maximum when marginal product is zero and TP starts falling when MP becomes negative (i.e. MP curve goes below the X-axis).

Three Phases of the Law

Fig. 3.1 clearly shows three phases of or three stages in the operation of the law of variable proportions. As we employ more units of the variable factor, the marginal product goes on increasing. The marginal product is maximum (QN) when ON units of the variable factor are employed. From point Q the marginal product starts declining but the average product continues to increase as long as the marginal product is more than the average product. At point P, both AP and MP are equal. At this point, stage I or the phase of *increasing returns* is over.

Employment of more than OA units of the variable factors marks the beginning of the second stage : the phase of *diminishing returns*. During this phase, both AP and MP are declining. This stage ends at point B where the marginal product is zero, and the total product is maximum.

The third stage starts after crossing the point B i.e. when more than OB units of the variable factor are employed. During this stage, the total product is declining. Employment of additional units of the variable factor in this stage does not help increase the output but actually causes a fall in total output.

Point A is said to denote the *extensive margin* which marks the end of increasing average returns, while point B is known as the *intensive margin* where employment of an additional unit of the variable factor stops adding anything to the total product.

Producer will not stop before OA units of the variable factor are employed, because average product per unit is increasing. He will not go beyond point B because it would mean inviting a fall in total product. Thus the point where he would stop (technically known as the point of equilibrium of the producer) will lie somewhere in stage II, i.e. between points A and B. Exact point of equilibrium will depend upon costs. Thus, in our example, if workers are willing to work free of charge, they will be employed till point B is reached. This is because every additional worker adds something to the total product but does not take anything for the work he does. As against this, the point of equilibrium will move towards A from B as wages increase. As long as marginal product is more than wage paid, it is to the advantage of the producer to employ additional workers.

An Explanation of the three Phases

It is essential to understand the behaviour of the average, the marginal and the total product through these three stages. During the first stage the average and the marginal products increase because of the following : (i) The fixed factor (e.g. a plant or a machine) is indivisible; and every addition in the variable factor means better utilization of the fixed factor. In our example, three hectares of (irrigated) land can be best cultivated with the help of 4 workers. So, as the number of workers is increased from 1 to 4, the fixed factors land a capital are better utilised. In other words, an increase in the efficiency of the fixed fact causes increasing returns in the first stage, (ii) With an increase in the employment of the variable factor, efficiency of the variable factor also increases due to the possibility of division of labour and specialisation. In our example, if four workers are employed every worker can be given the work for which he is the best suited. This is another reason why the average product increases.

During the second stage, diminishing returns are experienced because of the following factors : (i) The average product goes on increasing as long as the indivisible fixed factor get to the point of optimum utilisation. After this point, the fixed factor becomes inadequate relation to the variable factor and this causes a fall in the average product. In our example when the number of workers increases to 5 or more, the land (3 hectares) becomes inadequate for getting enough work done from so many workers, (ii) As pointed out by Mrs. Joa Robinson, *"there is a limit to the extent to which one factor of production can be substituted for another"*. In our example if the fifth worker had acted as a substitute for land i.e. if we had a option of say employing half a hectare of land or one worker, average product would have increased. But this is not possible. A workers cannot play the role of land. So the marginal an the average products start diminishing.

During the third stage, the occurrence of the negative marginal product and subsequent decline in the total product can be accounted for by the following factors : (i) With a continuou increase in the variable factor, we reach & stage when the number of units of that facto becomes too much for the fixed factor to cope with. Imagine, for example, a textile shop with a given space and a length of the counter. To begin with, an increase in the number of saiesmer will enable a better utilisation of the counter and specialisation - some salesman dealing with suiting and shirting, some others in saris and so on. But if the number of salesmen continue to increase, a stage will be reached when they will obstruct each others' movements and there will be no elbow-room. This will cause a negative marginal product i.e. total quantity of textiles sold will fall, (ii) Besides, too much increase in the variable factor puts a strain on the fixed factor also. This results in the erosion of the efficiency of the fixed factor causing a further fall in productivity.

3.4 RETURNS TO SCALE:

We shall now study production in the long run. In other words, we shall study the behaviour of output in response to a change in the scale. A change in the scale means that all factors of production are increased or decreased in the same proportion. Changes in scale is different from changes in factor proportions. Changes in output as a result of the variation in factor proportions, as seen before, form the subject matter of the law of variable proportions. On the other hand, the study of changes in output as a consequence of changes in scale forms the subject matter of returns to scale.

Returns to scale may be constant, increasing or decreasing. If we increase all factors i.e., scale in a given proportion and output increases in the same proportion, returns to scale are said to be constant. Thus if a doubling or trebling of all factors causes a doubling or trebling of output, returns to scale are constant. But if the increase in all factors leads to more than proportionate increase in output, returns to scale are said to be increasing. Thus if all factors are doubled and output increases more than a double then the returns to scale are said to be increasing. On the other hand if the increase in all factors leads to less than a proportionate increase in output, returns to scale are decreasing. This law operates in the long run when all the factors can be changed in some proportion simultaneously.

Constant returns to scale: As stated above, constant returns to scale means that with the increase in the scale in some proportion, output increases in the same proportion. In mathematics, the case of constant returns to scale is called linear homogeneous production function. Moreover, it has been found that production function for the economy as a whole corresponds to production function exhibiting constant returns to scale. Also, it has been found that an individual firm passes through a long phase of constant returns to scale in its lifetime. The Cobb-Douglas production function found out empirically (which applies to the manufacturing industry as a whole) also exhibits constant returns to scale.

Increasing returns to scale: Increasing returns to scale means that output increases in a greater proportion than the increase in inputs. When a firm expands, increasing returns to scale are obtained in the beginning. For example, a wooden box of 3 ft. cube contains 27 times greater wood than the wooden box of 1 foot-cube. Many such examples are found in real world. Another reason for increasing returns to scale is the indivisibility of factors. Some factors are available in large and lumpy units and can, therefore, be utilised with utmost efficiency at a large output. If all the factors are perfectly divisible, increasing returns may not occur.

Decreasing returns to scale: When output increases in a smaller proportion with an increase in all inputs, decreasing returns to scale are said to prevail. When a firm goes on expanding by increasing all inputs, then finally diminishing returns to scale set in. Some economists are of the view that an entrepreneur is a fixed factor of production; while other inputs may be increased, he cannot be. On this view, we get dimishing returns beyond a point because the variable quantities of all other inputs are combined with a fixed entrepreneur. Other economists do not treat decreasing returns to scale as a special case of the law of variable proportions and argue that decreasing returns to scale eventually occur because of increasing difficulties of management, coordination and control. When the firm has expanded to a very large size it is difficult to manage it with same efficiency as previously.

Table : Returns to Scale

Serial No. (in quintals)	Scale	TP (in quintals)	MPon returns
1	1W + 3A	2	2
2	2W +6A	5	3
3	3W +9A	9	4
4	4W +12A	14	5
5	5W + 15A	19	5
6	6W +18A	24	5
7	7W + 21A	28	4
8	8W + 24A	31	3
9	9W + 27A	33	2

W = Workers   and   A = Acres of Land

From the above table it is seen that, when we employ one worker oh 3 acres of land, TP is 2 quintals To increase output, when we double the scale, TP increases to more than double (5 quintals). MP increases by 3 quintals. When the scale is trebled, TP increases from 5 quintals to 9 quintals. MP increases from 3 quintals to 4 quintals. In other words the returns to scale has been increasing. If scale of production is further increased, MP remains constant upto a certain point and, beyond it, MP starts diminishing. With 9 workers being employed on 27 acres of land, MP declines to 2 quintals.

Returns to scale can also be explained with the help of the following Fig. 3.2

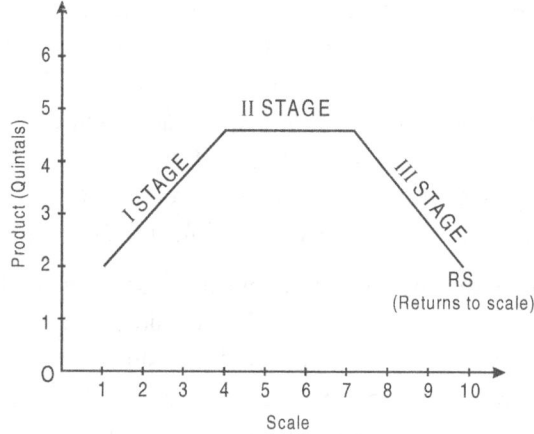

Fig. 3.2 : Returns to Scale

Explanation of the Three Stages of Returns to Scale :

When all the factors of production (labour, capital etc) are increased in a fixed proportion under the conditions of constant techniques, three production possibilities arise :

1. Increasing Returns to Scale :

This refers to a case when all factors of production are increased in a given proportion, output increases in a *greater* proportion. In the above example in Serial numbers 2, 3, 4, and 5, when the number of workers and acres of land are increased in a fixed proportion, i.e. the scale is doubled, trebled, made 4 times and 5 times, TP rises more than the rise in scale of operation. This can also be seen in terms of rising MP. There are two main factors which account for increasing returns to scale :

a. **Indivisibility :** The most important reason of increasing returns to scale is the 'technical and managerial indivisibilities'. The meaning of an indivisible factor of production is that there is a certain minimum size of the factor and even if it is large in relation to the size of the output, it has to be used (i.e. it cannot be divided). This means that most factors of production can be most efficiently employed at the outputs they were designed for and work less efficiently at smaller outputs because they cannot be divided into smaller units. They are indivisible. Plant cannot be used less fully without being used less economically. It is also indivisible. Accordingly, when the scale of operation is enlarged initially there is no equi-proportionate increase in the demand for the factors of production.

b. **Specialisation :** Increasing returns to scale may also occur because by increasing the scale of operation, *greater division of labour and specialization* becomes possible, i.e. each worker can specialize in performing a simple repetitive task rather than many different tasks. As a result, labour productivity increases. In addition, a larger scale of operation may permit the use of more productive specialized machinery which was not feasible at a lower scale of operation.

2. Constant Returns to Scale :

This means that if all factors of production are increased in a given proportion, the output produced increases in exactly the *same* proportion. In the above example, in Serial nos 5 and 6, when the number of workers and acres of land are increased in a fixed proportion, TP increases at a constant rate - from 14 quintals to 19 quintals and to 24 quintals, i.e. MP remains constant at 5 quintals. Such a production function is called a *linear homogeneous production function or homogeneous production function of the first degree.* The reasons which account for constant returns to scale are that, generally, when inefficiencies of production on a small scale are overcome and no problems regarding technical and managerial indivisibilities remain, expansion in scale leads to a situation where returns increase in the same proportion as the factors of production. Some economists are of the view that that when benefits of specialization of a factor in the unit of production are small or when such benefits have already been reaped at a small level of production, then for a considerable period of time production increases according to the law of constant returns to scale.

3. Diminishing Returns to Scale :

If output increases in a *smaller* proportion than the increase in all inputs there are decreasing or diminishing returns to scale. In the above example, in Serial Nos 7, 8, and 9, when the number of workers and acres of land are increased in a fixed proportion, TP increases at a diminishing rate - from 28 quintals to 31 quintals and to 33 quintals, i.e. MP decreases from 4 quintals, to 3 quintals and further to 2 quintals. Diminishing returns to scale ensure that the size of productive firms cannot be infinitely large. The operation of diminishing returns to scale is attributed to

a. **Indivisibility of enterprise :** Enterprise is a constant and indivisible factor of production and its supply cannot be increased even in the long run. Accordingly, when the quantity of other factors is increased and the scale of production expanded in a bid to boost up production, the proportion of other factors in relation to enterprise increases. Beyond a certain point, this results in diminishing returns as enterprise becomes scarce in relation to other factors;

b. **Managerial difficulties :** When the scale of operation expands, the co-ordination of and control on different factors of production tends to become weak. Communications difficulties may make it more and more difficult for the entrepreneur to run a business effectively. Therefore output fails to increase in the same proportion as the factors of production increase. This results in diminishing returns to scale.

Internal and External Economies and Diseconomies :

As a business expands the scale of its production (output) will increase, this in turn will influence the business production costs. If an increase in output results in lower unit costs it is known as economies of scale. If an increase in output results in higher unit costs it is known as diseconomies of scale.

Economies of Scale :

The concept "economies of scale" can be viewed in two senses : broad and narrow.

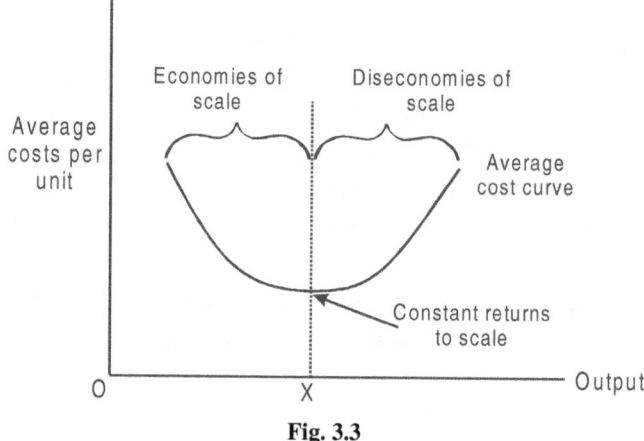

Fig. 3.3

In a broad sense anything which serves to minimize average cost of production in the long run as the scale of output increases is referred to as "economies of scale" It is measured in money terms.

In a narrow sense, the term "economies of scale" relates to the characteristics of the production process by which average productivity is enhanced with the expanding scale of output. Real economies are measured in physical terms. Increasing returns to scale are caused by these real economies.

The economies of scale may be classified as :
  I. Internal Economies.
  II. External Economies.

3.5 INTERNAL AND EXTERNAL ECONOMIES AND DISECONOMIES OF SCALE

Internal Economies and Diseconomies:

We saw that returns to scale increase in the initial stages and after remaining constant for a while, they decrease. The question arises as to why we get increasing returns to scale due to which cost falls and why after a certain point we get decreasing returns to scale due to which cost rises. The answer is that initially a firm enjoys internal economies of scale and beyond a certain limit it suffers from internal diseconomies of scale. **Internal economies and diseconomies** are of following main kinds:

(i) **Technical economies and diseconomies**: Large-scale production is associated with technical economies. As the firm increases its scale of operations, it becomes possible to use more specialised and efficient form of all factors, specially capital equipment and machinery. For producing higher levels of output, there is generally available a more efficient machinery which when employed to produce a large output yields a lower cost per unit of output. This happens due to indivisibility of capital equipment. If capital equipments were perfectly divisible, it would have been bought in required quantity and it would have been possible to produce the smallest output of any commodity with the advantages of large-scale production. Secondly, when the scale of production is increased and the amount of labour and other factors become larger, introduction of a greater degree of division of labour or specialisation becomes possible and as a result cost per unit declines.

However, beyond a certain point a firm experiences net diseconomies of scale. This happens because when the firm has reached a size large enough to allow utilisation of almost all the possibilities of division of labour and the employment of more efficient machinery, further increase in the size of the plant will entail high long-run cost because of difficulties of management. When the scale of operations becomes too large, it becomes difficult for the management to exercise control and to bring about proper coordination.

(ii) **Managerial economies and diseconomies**: These are economies arising out of specialization in the managerial functions of a firm. Managerial economies refer to reduction in managerial cost. When output increases, division of labour can be applied to management. The production manager can look after production, sales manager can look after sales, and finance manager can look after finance department. If scale of production increases further, each department can be further sub-divided lot e.g. sales can be split into sections for advertising exports and customer service.

Since individual activities come under the supervision of specialists, management's efficiency and productivity greatly improve. Decentralisation of decision making authority also becomes possible in such a firm which enhances further the efficiency and productivity of managers. Thus specialisation of management enables large firms to achieve reduction in managerial costs.

However, as scale of production increases beyond a certain limit, managerial diseconomies set in. Management finds it difficult to exercise control and bring coordination among various departments. The managerial structure becomes more cumbersome and is affected by more bureaucracy, more red tape, lengthening of communication lines and so on. All these affect the efficiency and productivity of management and the firm itself.

(ii) **Commercial economies and diseconomies**: These refer to the marketing economies enjoyed by a firm when it expands its scale of production. Production of big volumes of goods requires enough material and components. This enables the firm to place a bulk order for materials and components and enjoy lower prices for them. Economies can also be achieved in selling the product. Large firms can benefit from economies of advertising. As scale of production increases, advertising costs per unit of output fall..

Finally, when the business is sufficiently large, division of labour can be introduced on the commercial side, with expert buyers and sellers being employed.

These economies become diseconomies after an optimum scale. For example, advertisement expenditure and other marketing overheads will increase more than proportionately after the optimum scale.

(iv) Financial economic and diseconomies: In raising finance for expansion large firm is in favourable position. It can, for instance, offer better security to bankers and, because it is well-known, raise money at lower cost, since investors have confidence in it and prefer shares which can be readily sold on the stock exchange.

However, these financial costs will rise more proportionately after the optimum scale of production. This may happen because of relatively more dependence on external finances.

(v) Risk bearing economies and diseconomies: A firm is likely to face business risks i.e. economic ups and downs. A large firm is able to meet these business riks by diversifying its output, diversifting the markets and diversifying the source of supply of raw materials

However, risk may increase if diversification also fails.

External Economies and Diseconomies:

External economies and diseconomies are those economies and diseconomies which accrue to firms as a result of expansion in the output of whole industry and they are not dependent on the output level of individual firms. They are external in the sense they accrue to firms not out of their internal situation but from outside i.e. expansion of the industry. These are available to one or more of the firms in the form of:

1. **Cheaper raw materials and capital equipment:** The expansion of an industry may result in exploration of new and cheaper sources of raw material, machinery and other types of capital equipment. Expansion of, an industry results in greater demand for the various kinds of materials and capital equipment required by it. This makes it possible to purchase on a large scale from other industries. This reduces their cost of production and hence their prices. Thus, firms using these materials and capital equipment will be able to get them at a lower price.

2. **Technological external economies**: When the whole industry expands, it may result in the discovery of new technical knowledge and in accordance with that the use of improved and better machinery than before. This will enhance productivity of firms and reduce their cost of production.

3. **Development of skilled labour**: With the growth of an industry in an area a pool of trained labour equipped with the requisite skills is developed which has a favourable effect on the level of productivity and cost of the firms in that industry.

4. **Growth of ancillary industries**: With the growth of an industry, a number of ancillary industries may specialise in production of raw materials, tools and machinery etc. They can provide them at a lower price to the main industry. This will tend to reduce the cost of production in general.

5. **Better transportation and marketing facilities:** The expansion of an industry resulting from entry of new firms may make possible the development of transportation and marketing network to a great extent which will greatly reduce cost of production of the firms. Similarly, communication system may get modernised resulting in better and speedy information.

However, expansion of an industry may also result in some external diseconomies. An example of external diseconomies is the rise in some factor prices. When an industry expands, the requirement of the various factors of production increases; for example, that of all raw materials, capital goods, skilled labour and so on. This may result in pushing up the prices of such factors of production specially when they are short in supply. Moreover, too many firms in an industry at one place may also result in higher transportation cost, marketing cost and high pollution control cost. The government may also through its locational policy prohibit or restrict expansion of an industry at a particular place.

Exercise

1) Explain the Law of returns to scale.
2) Define total product, marginal product and average product.
3) State and illustrate with the help of a diagram the law of variable proportions.
4) What are the various internal economies and external economies of scale?

3.6 : COST ANALYSIS

Cost analysis refers to the study of behaviour of cost in relation to one or more' production criteria, namely, size of output, scale of operations, prices of factors of production and other relevant economic variables.

(A) TYPES OF COSTS

Accounting costs and economic costs:

When an entrepreneur undertakes an act of production he has to pay prices for the factors which he employs for production. He thus pays wages to workers employed, prices for the raw materials, fuel and power used, rent for the building he hires, and interest on the money borrowed for doing business. All these are included in his cost of production and are termed as accounting costs.

It generally happens that an entrepreneur invests a certain amount of capital in his productive business. If the capital invested by the entrepreneur in his business had been invested elsewhere it would have earned certain amount of interest or dividend. Moreover, an entrepreneur devotes time to his own work of production and contributes his entrepreneurial and managerial ability to do business. Had he not set up his own business he would have sold his services to others for some positive amount of money. Accounting costs do not include these costs. These costs form a part of the economic cost.

Thus accounting costs relate to those costs only which involve cash payments by the entrepreneur of the firm. Accounting costs are also called explicit costs.

Economic costs include: (1) the normal return on money capital invested by the entrepreneur himself in his own business; (2) the wages or salary not paid to the entrepreneur but could have been earned if the services had been sold somewhere else. The cost of factors owned by the entrepreneur himself and employed in his own business are called implicit costs. Thus economic costs include both accounting (explicit) costs and implicit costs. The concept of economic cost is important because an entrepreneur must cover his economic cost if he wants to earn normal profits and abnormal profits are over and above these normal profits.

Outlay costs and opportunity costs :

Outlay costs involve actual outlay of funds on, say, wages, material, rent, interest, etc. Opportunity cost, on the other hand, is concerned with the cost of foregone opportunity. It involves a comparison between the policy that was chosen and the policy that was" rejected. For example, the cost of lending or using capital is the interest that it can earn in the next best use of equal risk.

A distinction between outlay costs and opportunity costs can be drawn on the basis of the nature of the sacrifice. Outlay costs involve financial expenditure at some time and hence are recorded in the books of account. Opportunity costs relate to sacrificed alternatives; they are not recorded in the books of account in general.

In long-term cost calculation also it is useful e.g., in calculating the cost of higher education, it is not the tuition fee and books but the earning foregone that should be taken into account.

Direct or traceable costs and indirect or non-traceable costs :

Direct costs are costs that are readily identified and are traceable to a particular product, operation or plant. Even overhead can be direct as to a department; manufacturing costs can be direct to a product line, sales territory, customer class etc. We must know the purpose of cost calculation before considering whether a cost is direct or indirect.

Indirect costs are not readily identified nor visibly traceable to specific goods, services, operations, etc. but are nevertheless charged to the jobs or products in standard accounting practice. Examples of such costs are electric power, the common costs incurred for general operation of business benefiting all products jointly.

Fixed and variable costs :

Fixed or constant costs are not a function of output; they do not vary with output upto a certain level of activity. These costs require a fixed outlay of funds irrespective of the level of output, e.g., rent, property taxes, interest on loans, depreciation when taken as a function of time and not of output. However, these costs also vary with the size of the plant and are a function of capacity. Therefore, fixed costs do not vary with the volume of output within a capacity level.

Fixed costs cannot be avoided. These costs are fixed so long as operations are going on. They can be avoided only when operations are completely closed down. We can call them as inescapable or uncontrollable costs.

Variable costs are costs that are a function of output in the production period. Variable costs vary directly and sometimes proportionately with output. Over certain ranges of production they may vary less or more than proportionately depending on the utilisation of fixed facilities and resources in the process of production.

Shutdown and abandonment costs :

Shutdown costs may be those which would be incurred in the event of a temporary cessation of business activities and which could be saved if operations were allowed to continue. Shutdown costs, besides fixed costs, cover the additional expenses in looking after the property not disposed of.

Abandonment costs are the cost of retiring a fixed asset from use. For example, a second hand plant installed in war time may not be useful during peace time. Abandonment thus involves permanent cessation of activity and raises the problem of disposal of assets.

B) BEHAVIOUR OF COST CURVES

(1) Short run cost Analysis

Total, fixed and variable costs: There are some factors which can be easily adjusted with changes in the level of output. Thus a firm can readily employ more workers if it has to increase output. Similarly, it can purchase more raw material if it has to expand production. Such factors which can be easily varied with a change in the level of output are called variable factors. On the other hand, there are factors such as building, capital equipment, or top management team which cannot be so easily varied. It requires comparatively longer time to make changes in them. It takes time to install a new machinery. Similarly, it takes time to build a new factory. Such factors which cannot be readily varied and require a longer period to adjust are called fixed factors. Corresponding to the distinction between variable and fixed factors we distinguish between short run and long run periods of time. Short run is a period of time in which output can be increased or decreased by changing only the amount of variable factors, such as labour, raw material etc. In the short run, quantities of fixed factors cannot be varied in accordance with changes in output. If the firm wants to increase output in the short run, it can do so only with the help of variable factors, i.e., by using more labour and/or by buying more raw material. Thus, short run is a period of time in which only variable factors can be varied, while the quantities of fixed factors remain unaltered. On the other hand, long run is a period of time in which the quantities of all factors may be varied. Thus all factors become variable in the long run.

Thus we find that fixed costs are those costs which are independent of output, i.e., they do not change with changes in output. These costs are a "fixed amount" which are incurred by a firm in the short run, whether the output is small or large. Even if the firm closes down for some time in the short run but remains in business, these costs have to be borne by it. Fixed costs include such charges as contractual rent, insurance fee, maintenance cost, property taxes, interest on capital employed, manager's salary, watchman's wages etc. Variable costs on the other hand are those costs which change with changes in output. These costs include payments such as wages of labour employed, prices of raw material, fuel and power used, transportation cost etc. If a firm shuts down for a short period, then it may not use variable factors of production and will not therefore incur any variable cost.

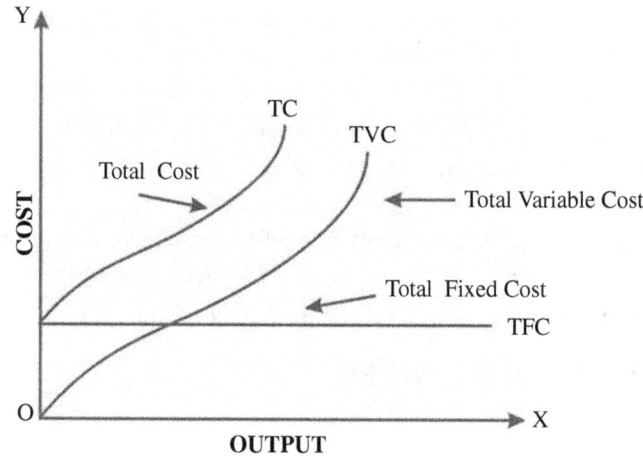

Fig. 3.4 : Short-run Total Cost Curves

Total cost of a business is thus the sum of total variable cost and total fixed cost or symbolically

$$TC = TFC + TVC.$$

We may also represent total cost, total variable cost and fixed cost diagrammatically.

In the above diagram, total fixed cost curve (TFC) is parallel to X- axis. This curve starts from the point on the Y-axis meaning thereby that fixed cost will be incurred even if the output is zero. On the other hand total variable cost one rises upward showing thereby that as output increases, total variable cost also increases. This curve starts from the origin which shows that when the output is zero, variable costs are also nil. The total cost curve has been obtained by adding vertically total fixed cost curve and total variable cost curve.

Short run average cost

Average fixed cost (AFC): AFC is the total fixed cost divided by the number of units of output produced, i.e.

$$AFC = \frac{TFC}{Q}$$

where Q is the number of units produced. Thus average fixed cost is the fixed cost per unit of output. For example, a firm is producing with total fixed cost at Rs. 1,000/-. When output is 100 units, average fixed cost will be Rs. 10/-. And now if the output increases to 200 units, average fixed cost will be Rs. 5/-. Since total fixed cost is a constant amount; average fixed cost will steadily fall as output increases. Therefore, if we draw average fixed cost curve, it will slope downwards throughout its length. (Fig. 3.4)

Average variable cost (AVC): Average variable cost is the total variable cost divided by the number of units of output produced, i.e. $AVC = \dfrac{TVC}{Q}$ where Q is the number of units produced. Thus average variable cost is variable cost per unit of output. Average variable cost normally falls as output increases from zero to normal capacity output due to occurrence of increasing returns. But beyond the normal capacity output, average variable cost will rise steeply because of the operation of diminishing returns If we draw average variable cost curve it will first fall, then reach a minimum and then rise again. (Fig. 3.5)

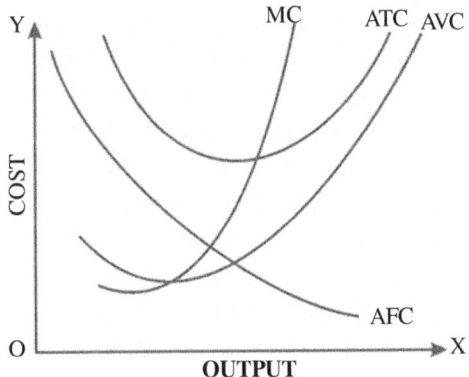

Fig. 3.5 : Short-run Average and Marginal Cost Curves

Average total cost (ATC): Average total cost is a sum of average variable cost and average fixed cost, i.e., ATC = AFC + AVC. It is the total cost divided by the number of units produced. The behaviour of average total cost curve depends upon the behaviour of average variable cost curve and average fixed cost curve. In the beginning both AVC and AFC curves fall, therefore, the ATC curve will also fall sharply in the beginning. When AVC curve begins to rise, but AFC curve still falls steeply, ATC curve continues to fall. This is because during this stage the fall in AFC curve is greater than the rise in the AVC curve but as output increases further, there is a sharp rise in AVC which more than offsets the fall in AFC. Therefore, ATC curve first falls, reaches its minimum and then rises. Thus, the average total cost curve is "U" shape curve. (Fig. 3.5)

Marginal Cost: Marginal cost is the addition made to the total cost by production of an additional unit of output. In other words, it is the total cost of producing t units instead of t-1 units, where t is any given number. For example, if we are producing 5 units at a cost of Rs. 200

and now suppose 6th unit is produced and the total cost is Rs. 250, marginal cost is Rs. 250 - 200 i.e., Rs. 50/-. It is to be noted that marginal cost is independent of fixed cost. This is because fixed costs do not change with output. It is only the variable costs which change with a change in the level of output in the short run. Therefore, marginal cost is in fact due to the changes in variable costs.

Marginal cost curve falls as output increases in the beginning. It starts rising after a certain level of output. This happens because of the influence of the law of variable proportions. The fact that marginal product rises first, reaches a maximum and then declines ensures that the marginal cost curve of a firm declines first, reaches its minimum and then rises. In other words marginal cost curve of a firm is "U" shaped (see Figure 3.5).

The behaviour of these costs has also been shown in Table 1.

Table 1 : Various Costs

Units of output	Total fixed cost	Total variable cost	Total cost	Average fixed cost	Average variable cost	Average total cost	Marginal cost per unit
0	150	0	150	–	–	–	–
6	150	50	200	25.0	8.33	33.33	$\frac{50}{6} = 8.33$
16	150	100	250	9.38	6.25	15.63	$\frac{50}{10} = 5.00$
29	150	150	300	5.17	5.17	10.34	$\frac{50}{13} = 3.85$
44	150	200	350	3.41	4.55	7.95	$\frac{50}{15} = 3.33$
55	150	250	400	2.73	4.55	7.27	$\frac{50}{11} = 4.55$
60	150	300	450	2.50	5.00	7.50	$\frac{50}{5} = 10.00$

The above table shows that:

(i) Fixed cost does not change with increase in output upto a given range. Average fixed cost, therefore, comes down with every increase in output,

(ii) Variable cost increases but not necessarily in the same proportion as the increase in output. In the above case, average variable cost comes down gradually till 55 units are produced.

(iii) Marginal cost is the additional cost divided by addition units produced. This also comes gradually till 44 units are produced.

Relationship between Average Cost and Marginal Cost: The following are the points of relationship between the Average and Marginal costs.

(1) When average cost falls as a result of an increase in output, marginal cost is less than average cost.

(2) When average cost rises as a result of an increase in output, marginal cost is more than average cost.

(3) When average cost is minimum, marginal cost is equal to the average cost. In other words, marginal cost curve cuts average cost curve at its minimum point (i.e. optimum point).

Long Run Average Cost Curves

As stated above long run is a period of time during which the firm can vary all of its inputs-unlike short run in which some inputs are fixed and others are variable. In other words, whereas in the short run the firm is tied with given plant, in the long run the firm moves from one plant to another; it can acquire a big plant if it wants to increase its output and a small plant if it wants to reduce its output. Long run cost of production is the least possible cost of producing any given level of output when all individual factors are variable. A long run cost curve depicts the functional relationship between output and the long run cost of production.

In order to understand how long run average cost curve is derived we consider three short run average cost curves as shown in Figure 3.6. These short run cost curves (SACs) are also called plant curves. In the short run the firm can be operating on any short run average cost curve given the size of the plant. Suppose that these are the only three plants which are technically possible. Given the size of the plant, the firm will be increasing or increasing its output by changing the amount of the variable inputs. But in the long run, the firm chooses among the three possible sizes of plants as depicted by short run average curve (SAC_1, SAC_2, SAC_3). In the long run, the firm will examine with which size of plants or on which short average cost curve it should operate to produce a given level of output so that total cost is minimum. It will be seen from the diagram that upto OB amount of output the firm will operate on the SAC_1, though it could also produce with SAC_2, because upto OB amount of output, the production on SAC_1 results in lower cost than on SAC_2. For example, if the level of output OA is produced with SAC_1, it will cost AL per unit and if it is produced with SAC_2 it will cost AH and we can see that AH is more than AL. Similarly, if the firm plans to produce an output which is larger than OB but less than OD then it will not be economical to produce on SAC_1. For this, the firm will have to use SAC_2. Similarly, the firm will use SAC_3 for output larger than OD. It is thus clear that in the long run the firm has a choice in the employment of plant and it will employ that plant which yields minimum possible unit cost for producing a given output.

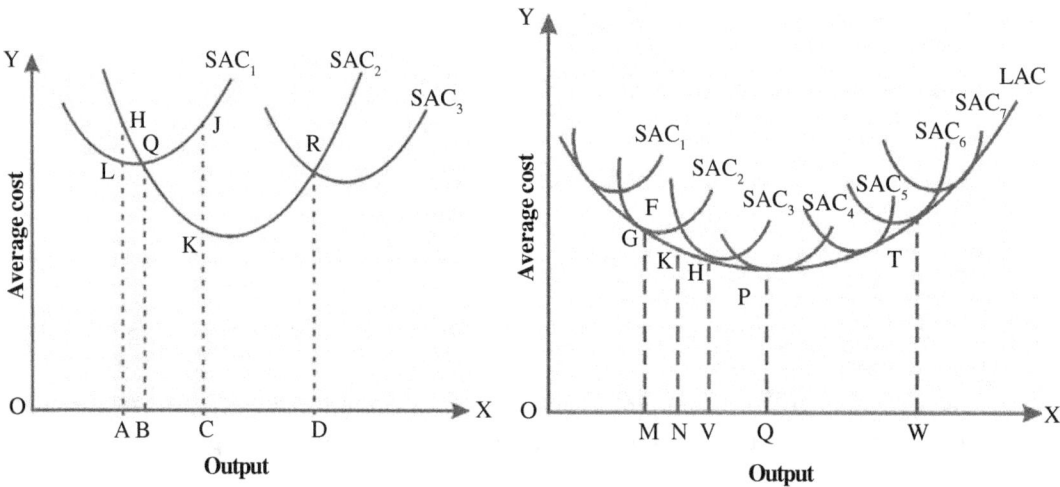

Fig. 3.6: Short-run Average Cost Curves   Fig. 3.7: Long-run Average Cost Curve

Suppose now, the firm has a choice so that a plant can be varied by infinitely small gradations so that there are infinite number of plants corresponding to which there numerous average cost curves. In such a case the long run average cost curve will be a smooth curve enveloping all these short run average cost curves.

As shown in Figure 3.7 the long run average cost curve is so drawn as to be tangent to each of the short run average cost curves. Every point on the long run average cost curve will be a tangency point with some short run AC curve. If a firm desires to produce any particular output it then builds a corresponding plant and operate on the corresponding short run average cost curve. As shown in the figure, for producing OM the corresponding point on the LAC curve is G and the short run average cost curve SAC$_2$ is tangent to the long run AC at this point. Thus if a firm desires to produce output OM, the firm will construct a plant corresponding to SAC$_2$ and will operate on this curve at point G. Similarly, the firm will produce other levels of output choosing the plant which suits its requirements of lowest possible cost of production. It is clear from the figure that the large output can be produced at the lowest cost with the larger plant whereas smaller output can be produced at the lowest cost with smaller plants. For example, to produce OM, the firm will be using SAC$_2$ only; if it uses SAC$_3$ for this, it will result in higher unit cost than SAC$_2$. But larger output OV can be produced most economically with a larger plant represented by the SAC$_3$. If we produce OV with the smaller plant it will result in higher unit cost. This happens because if we employ a larger plant to produce a small output it will not be fully utilised; similarly if we produce larger output with a smaller plant it will involve higher cost because of its limited capacity.

It is to be noted that LAC curve is not a tangent to the minimum points of the SAC curves. When the LAC curve is declining it is tangent to the falling portions of the short run cost curves and when the LAC curve is rising it is tangent to the rising portions of the short run cost curves. Thus for producing output less than "OQ" at the lowest possible unit cost the firm will construct the relevant plant and operate it at less than its full capacity, i.e., at less than its minimum average cost of production. On the other hand for output larger than ie firm will construct a plant and operate it beyond its optimum capacity. "OQ" is the optimum output. This is because "OQ" is being produced at the minimum point of LAC and corresponding SAC i.e., SAC_4 Other plants are either used at less than their full capacity or more than their full capacity. Only SAC_4 is being   at the minimum point.

Long run average cost curve is often called a planning curve because a firm plans to produce any output in the longrun by choosing a plant on the long run average cost curve corresponding to the given output. The long run average cost curve helps the firm in the choice of the size of the plant for producing a specific output at the least possible cost.

Explanation of the "U" shape of the long run average cost curve:

As has been seen in the diagram LAC cune is a "U" shape curve. This shape of LAC curve depends upon the returns to scale. As discussed earlier, as the firm expands returns to scale increase. After a range of constant returns to scale, the returns to scale finally decrease. On the same line, the LAC curve first declines and then finally rises. Increasing returns to scale cause fall in the long run average cost and decreasing returns to scale result in increase in long run average cost. Falling long run average cost and increasing economies to scale result from internal and external economies of scale and rising long run average cost and diminishing returns to scale from internal and external diseconomies of scale (economies of scale have been discussed earlier at the relevant place).

Exercise

1) Define opportunity cost marginal cost.
2) Distinguish between economic cost and accounting cost.
3) State the relationship between average cost and marginal cost.
4) Show how the long run average cost curve is derived with the help of short run average cost curves.
5) Explain why the average cost curve is U-shaped.

Revenue Behaviour

Contents

4.1 INTRODUCTION

Market demand is determined by adding up the various quantities demanded by individual buyers in the market. Demand would be higher at a lower price and the same would be lower at a higher price. Producers or sellers of goods are also concerned with the demand for a good because revenues obtained by them from selling the goods mainly depend on the demand for goods. Total number of units sold multiplied by the selling price per unit would give the total revenue earned by the firm. Hence, a firm's revenue would reflect the demand for its product in the market. It is , therefore, necessary to understand the revenue concepts for analyzing the process of price determination and the equilibrium of the firm.

4.2 CONCEPTS OF TOTAL REVENUE, AVERAGE REVENUE, MARGINAL REVENUE

Total Revenue (TR): TR refers to the amount of money which a firm realizes by selling certain units of a commodity. If a firm sells 100 units for Rs.20 each, what is the amount which it realises? It realises Rs. 2,000 (100 units × Rs.20), which is nothing but total revenue for the firm. Symbolically, total revenue may be expressed as

TR = P × Q

Where,   TR is total revenue

P is price

Q is Quantity of a commodity sold

Average Revenue (AR) :

Average revenue is the revenue earned per unit of output. It is nothing but price of one unit of output because price is always per unit of a commodity. Symbolically, average revenue is :

$$AR = \frac{TR}{Q}$$

Where   AR is average revenue
            TR is the total revenue
            Q is quantity of a commodity sold

or
$$AR = \frac{P \times Q}{Q}$$

or
$$AR = P$$

If, for example, a firm realises total revenue of Rs. 2,000 by the sale of 100 units. It implies that the average revenue is Rs.20 (Rs.2 ,000/100 units) or the firm has sold the commodity at a price of Rs.20 per unit.

Marginal Revenue :

Marginal revenue (MR) is the change in total revenue resulting from the sale of an additional unit of the commodity. Thus if a seller realises Rs. 1,000 after selling 100 units and Rs. 1,200 after selling 101 units, we say marginal revenue is Rs.200. We can say that MR is-the rate of change in total revenue resulting from the sale of an additional unit.

$$MR = \frac{\Delta TR}{\Delta Q}$$

Where   MR is marginal revenue
            TR is total revenue
            Q is quantity of a commodity sold
            Δ is the rate of change.

For one unit change in output
$$MR_n = TR_n - TR_{n-1}$$

Where
            TR is the total revenue when sales are at the rate of n units per period.
            TR_{n-1} is the total revenue when sales are at the rate of n - 1 unit per period.

4.3 RELATIONSHIP BETWEEN TOTAL REVENUE, AVERAGE REVENUE AND MARGINAL REVENUE

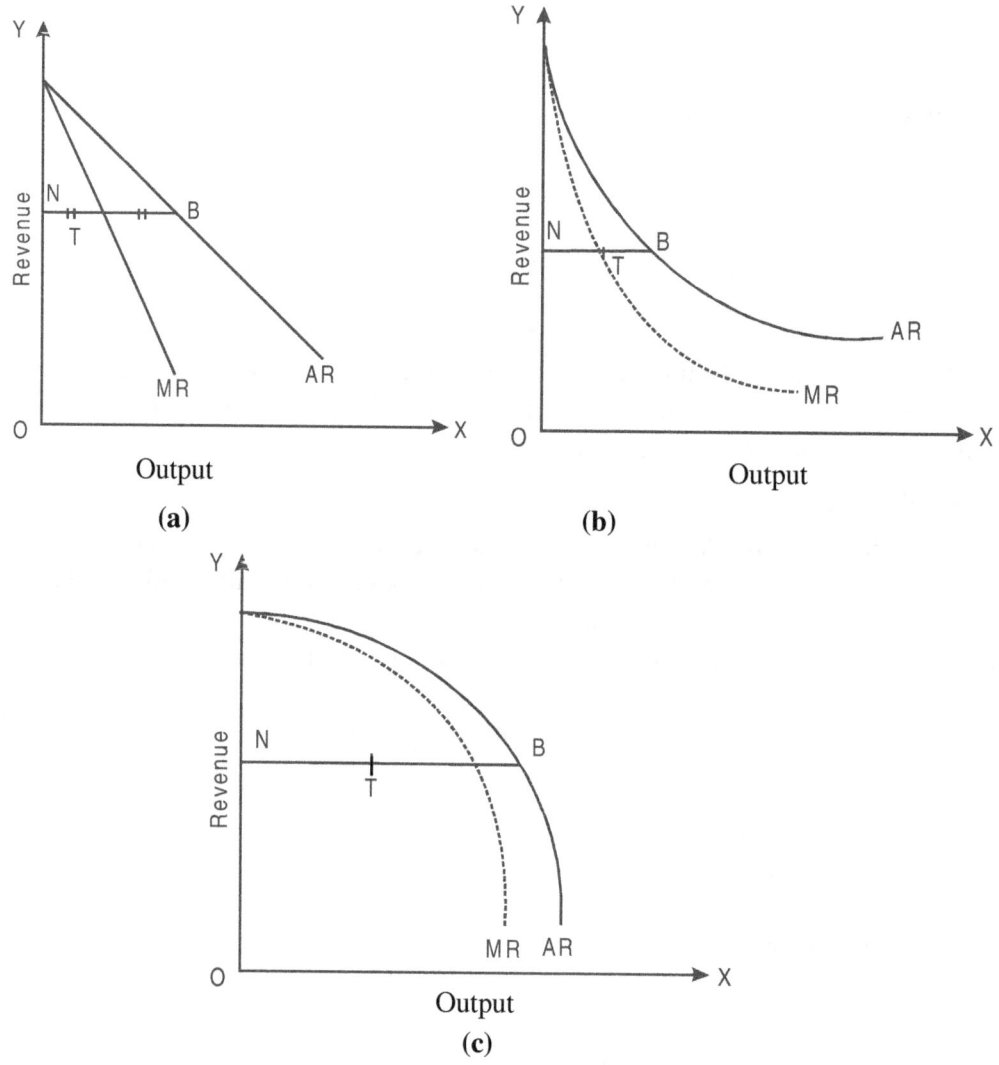

Fig. 4.1: Revenue Relationships

In figure 4.1 *(a)*, (b), and (c) we find three possible shapes of AR and MR curves. The curves may either be straight lines as in Fig. 4.1 (a) or convex to the origin, as in Fig. 4.1 (b) or concave to the origin, as in Fig. 4.1 (c). Table 4.1 and Fig. 4.1 (a), (b), and *(c)* show the relationships between average revenue, marginal revenue and total revenue. These relationships can be summarised *as* follows :

(i) Marginal revenue is the addition to the total revenue, while average revenue is the price of the product.

(ii) When supply of a product is increased, price per unit decreases. Under conditions of perfect competition the price remains constant. That is why under competitive conditions the price or average revenue remains constant whatever the level of output produced by a single firm.

Alternatively, when the firm is producing under the conditions of imperfect competition, price or average revenue declines as the supply increases. Thus, under no conditions will the price rise as supply of a firm increases. Therefore, the average and marginal revenues will either fall or remain constant but never rise, as the market supply of a product produced by a firm increases.

(iii) When average revenue is constant, i.e. it does not change along with an increase or decrease in output, marginal revenue or addition to total revenue is also constant. Under such conditions, AR and MR are equal.

Table 4.2 illustrates this point. Since AR is constant at Rs. 10, MR is also constant at Rs. 10 and thus, both AR and MR are equal and constant. This is the nature of AR and MR of a firm producing under conditions of perfect competition.

Figure 4.2, shows constants AR and MR, at all levels of output. As output increases from OQ_1 to OQ_2 and further to OQ_3 marginal revenue remains the same $(Q_1P_1 = Q_2P_2 = Q_3P_3)$

Table 4.1 : Constant Revenue

Output(Units)	AR(Rs.)	TR (Rs.)	MR(Rs.)
1	10	10	10
2	10	20	10
3	10	30	10
4	10	40	10
5	10	50	10

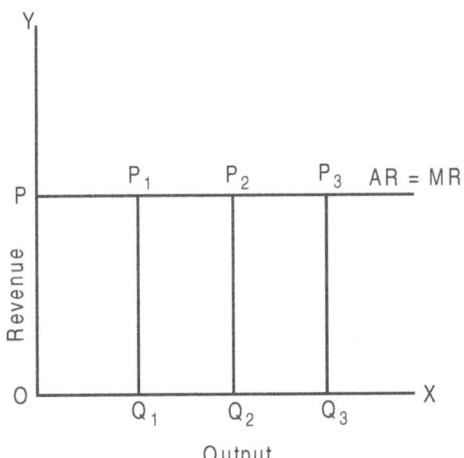

Fig. 4.2 : Average and Marginal Revenues of a competitive form

That is why AR = MR curve of a firm is parallel to X-axis, under conditions of perfect competition, as shown in Fig. 4.2.

(iv) When average revenue is falling marginal revenue is less than average revenue falls more steeply, so that the gap between the two widens as output increases. This would be clear from table 4.1.

(v) When AR and MR curves are straight lines, the MR curve bisects the perpendicular drawn from any point on the average revenue curve to the Y-axis. In Fig. 4.1 (a), AR and MR are straight lines, BN is the perpendicular drawn from any point B on the AR curve to the Y-axis. The MR curve bisects BN in such a way that NT = TB. When AR curve is convex to the origin as in Fig. 4.1 (b), the MR curve cuts the perpendicular drawn to Y-axis from any point on the AR curve, at a point which would be to the left of the mid-point T. In other words, the MR curve which is convex to the origin will intersect the NB line through NT section. Alternatively, when AR is concave to the origin, the MR curve cuts the perpendicular drawn to Y-axis from any point on AR through a point which is to the right of the mid-point of the perpendicular. In other words, the MR would cut NB in TB portion as shown in Fig. 4.1 (c).

(vi) As long as marginal revenue is positive, total revenue continues to increase. Total revenue will stop increasing and start decreasing, the moment marginal revenue falls below zero and becomes negative.

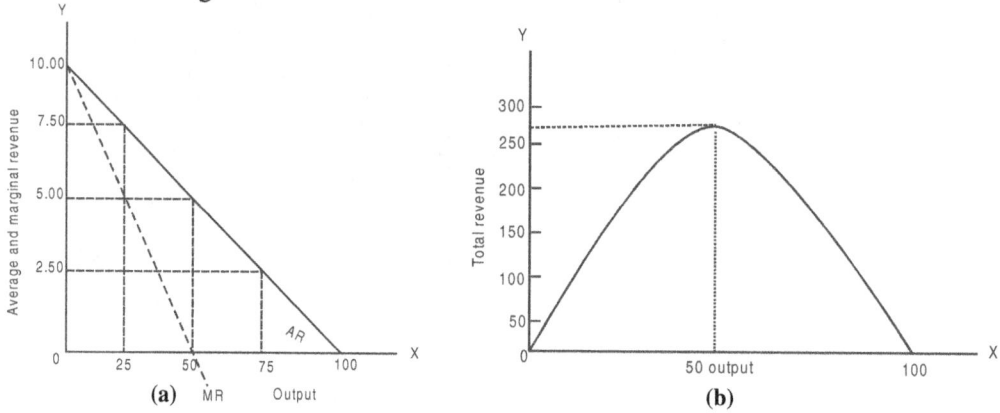

Fig. 4.3 : AR, MR and TR under Monopoly

(vii) Total revenue will be maximum at a point where marginal revenue is zero. This is shown in Fig. 4.3 (a) and (b). Fig. 4.3 (a) and (b), shows AR and MR relationships under conditions of monopoly. At 50 units of output, marginal revenue is zero as shown in Fig. 4.3 (a). At this level of output, i.e. when the total output *is* 50 units, total revenue is maximum i.e. Rs. 275 as shown in Fig. 4.3 (b).

Exercise

1. Define Total Revenue, Average Revenue and Marginal Revenue.
2. Explain the relationship between Total Revenue, Average Revenue and Marginal Revenue.

Pricing Under Various Market Conditions

Contents

5.1 INTRODCTION

The concept of price especially the process of price determination is of vital importance in economics. Output is supplied by individual firms on the basis of market demand, their cost and revenue functions. However, the existence of different forms of market structure leads to differences in demand and revenue functions of the firms. Therefore, supplies offered at different prices by the firm would vary significantly depending upon the market forms. We shall study the determination of price and output under perfect competition, monopoly, monopolistic competition and oligopoly.

5.2 PERFECT COMPETITION

It is the simplest form of market structure. It is an ideal market structure that seldom exists in the real world. However, the situation of perfectly competitive market provides the base, which helps in the price output determination in different market forms.

Features

A perfectly competitive market exists when the market shows following characteristics:

1) **Large number of Buyers and Sellers** : There are *a* large number of buyers and sellers who compete among themselves and their number is so large that no buyer or seller is in a position to influence the demand or supply in the market.

2) **Homogeneous Product :** The commodity dealt in it is homogeneous in the sense that the goods produced by different firms are identical in nature. It implies that in a perfectly competitive market the product of anyone firm is a perfect substitute of the product of any other firm

3) **Free Entry and Exit :** Every firm is free to enter the market or leave the market. There should be no constraints on firms which want to come into or go out of business.

If the above three conditions alone are fulfilled, then it is called **PURE COMPETITION.**

In addition to the above three conditions, some more conditions are attached to perfect competition. These are as follows :

4) **Perfect Knowledge of the market :** There is a perfect knowledge, on the part of buyers and sellers, of the quantities of stock of goods in the market, market conditions and the prices at which transactions of purchase and sale are being entered into. As a result uniform price prevails in the market. Because there is perfect knowledge of the market, no seller will accept a price lower than that ruling in the market, nor will any buyer offer a price higher than the market price.

5) **Perfect Mobility of Factors of Production** : In perfect competition, all factors of production are mobile. Facilities exist for the movement of goods from one centre to another. Also buyers have no preference as between different sellers and as between different units of commodity offered for sale; also sellers are quite indifferent as to whom they sell.

6) **Uniform Price :** The commodity or the goods are dealt on at a uniform price throughout the market at a given point of time. In other words, all firms individually are price takers; they have to accept the price determined by the market forces to total demand and total supply.

While there are few examples of perfect competition, which is regarded as a myth by many, the grain or stock markets approach the condition of perfect competition.

Price determination under perfect competition

Equilibrium of the Industry: Industry is the group of producers or firms.. Each such unit in the industry produces a homogeneous product so that there is competition amongst goods produced by different units called firms. When the total output of the industry is equal to the total demand we say that the industry is in equilibrium; the price then prevailing is equilibrium price, whereas a firm is said to be in equilibrium when it has no incentive to expand or contract production.

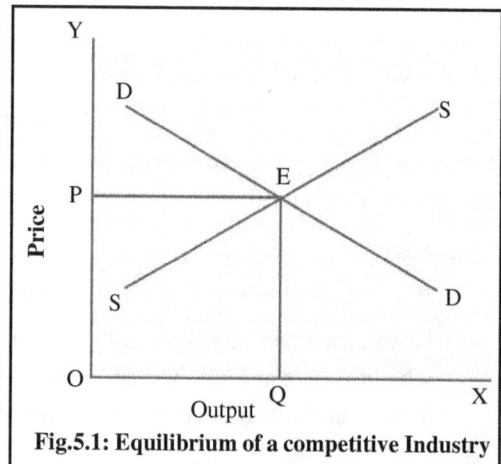

Fig.5.1: Equilibrium of a competitive Industry

As stated above under competitive conditions, the equilibrium price for a given product is determined by the interaction of forces of demand and supply for it as is shown in figure 5.1.

In Fig. 5.1, OP is the equilibrium price and OQ is the equilibrium quantity which will be sold at that price. The equilibrium price is the price at which both the demand and supply are equal at which no buyer goes dissatisfied who wanted to buy at that price and none of the sellers is dissatisfied that he could not sell his goods at that price. It will be noticed that if price were to be fixed at any other level, higher or lower, demand remaining the same, there would not be equilibrium in the market. Likewise, if the quantities of goods were greater or smaller than the demand, there would not be equilibrium.

Equilibrium of the Firm :

The firm is said to be in equilibrium when it maximises its profit. The output which gives maximum profit to the firm is called equilibrium output. In the equilibrium state, the firm has no incentive either to increase or decrease its output. Since it is the maximum profit giving output which only gives no incentive to the firm to increase or decrease it, so it is in equilibrium when it gets maximum profit.

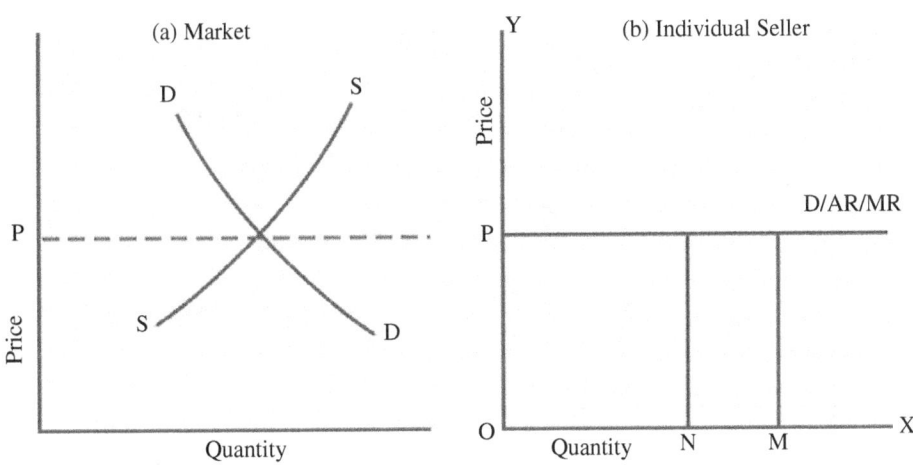

Fig 5.2 : The firm's demand curve under perfect competition

Firms in a competitive market are price-takers. This is because there are a large number of firms in the market who are producing identical or homogeneous products. As such these firms cannot influence the price in their individual capacities. They have to accept the price fixed (through interaction of total demand and total supply) by the industry as a whole. Industry price OP is fixed through the interaction of total demand and total supply of the industry. Firms have to accept this price as given and as such they are price-takers rather than price makers. They cannot increase the price OP alone because of the fear of losing customers to other firms. They do not try to sell the product below OP because they do not have any incentive for lowering it. They will try to sell as much as they can at price OP.

As such P-line acts as a demand curve for them. Thus the demand curve facing an individual firm in a perfectly competitive market is horizontal one at the level of market price set by the industry and firms have to choose that level of output which yields maximum profit. Let us take an example in which demand and supply schedule for the industry are as follows:

Table 1 : Equilibrium price for industry

Price (units)	Demand (Units)	Supply (Units)
1	40	50
2	35	35
3	20	45
4	15	55
5	10	65

Equilibrium price for the industry thus fixed through the interaction of the demand and supply is Rs.2 per unit. The individual firms will accept Rs.2 per unit as the price and sell different quantities at this price. Let us consider the case of firm 'X'. Firm X's quantity sold, total revenue, average revenue and marginal revenue are given in Table 2:

Table 2: Trends of Revenue for the Firm

Price (Rs.)	Quantity Sold	Total Revenue	Average Revenue	Marginal Revenue
2	8	16	2	2
2	10	20	2	2
2	12	24	2	2
2	14	28	2	2
2	16	32	2	2

Firm X's price, average revenue and marginal revenue is equal to Rs.2. Thus we see that in a perfectly competitive market a firm's AR = MR = price.

Conditions for equilibrium of a firm:

As discussed earlier, a firm in order to attain the equilibrium position has to satisfy two conditions:

(1) The marginal revenue should be equal to the marginal cost. i.e. MR = MC. If MR is greater than MC, there is always an incentive for the firm to expand its production further and gain by sale of additional units. If MR is less than MC, the firm will have to reduce output since an additional unit adds more to cost than to revenue. Profits are maximum only at the point where MR = MC.

(2) The MC curve should cut MR curve from below. In other words, MC should have positive slope.

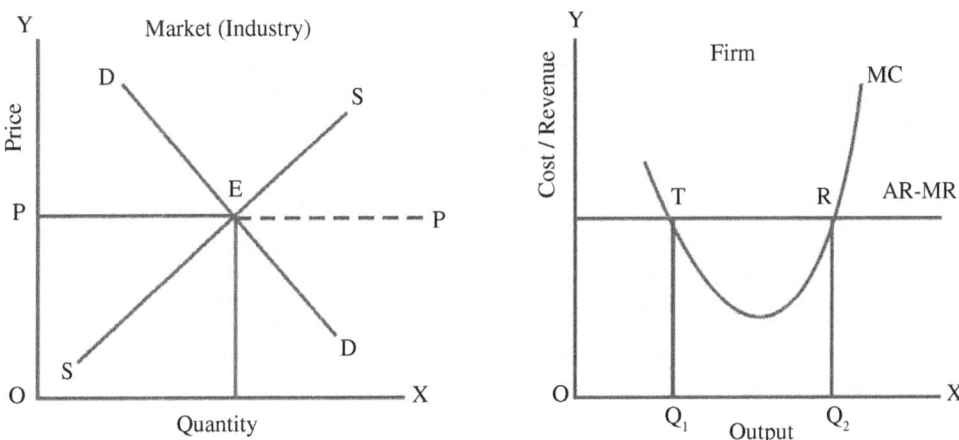

Fig. 5.3 : Equilibrium position for a firm under perfect competition

In figure 5.3, DD and SS are the industry demand and supply curves which equilibrate at E to set the market price as OP. The firms of perfectly competitive industry adopt OP price as given and considers P-Line as demand (Average revenue) curve which is perfectly elastic at P. As all the units are priced at the same level, MR is a horizontal line equal to AR line. Note that MC curve cuts MR curve at two places T and R respectively. But at T, the MC curve is cutting MR curve from above. T is not the point of equilibrium as the second condition is not satisfied. The firm will benefit if it goes beyond T as the additional cost of producing additional unit is falling. At R, the MC curve is cutting MR curve from below. Hence R is the point of equilibrium OQ_2 is equilibrium level of output.

Supply curve of the firm in a competitive market:

One interesting thing about the MC curve of the firm in a perfectly competitive industry is that it depicts the firm's supply curve. This can be shown with the help of the following example.

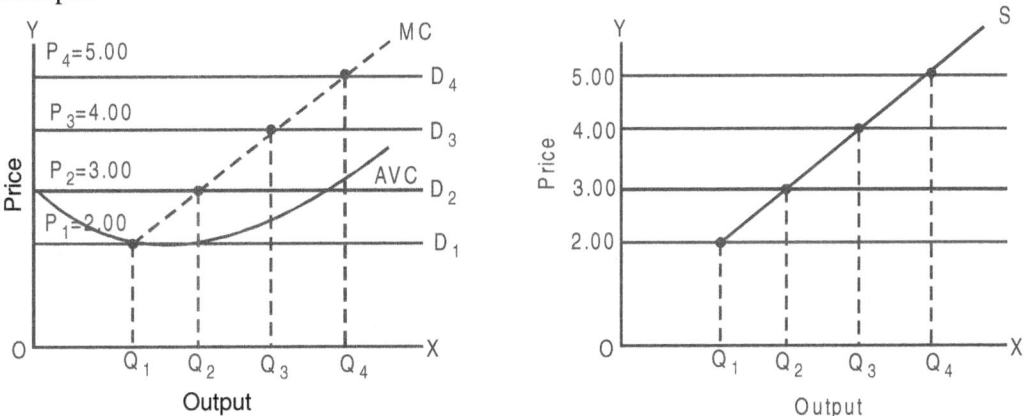

Fig 5.4 : Marginal cost and Supply curves for Price-taking firm

Suppose market price of a product is Rs.2 corresponding to it we have D, as demand curve for the firm. At price Rs.2, the firm supplies Q1 output because here MR=MC. If the market price is Rs.3, the corresponding demand curve is D_2. At Rs.3, the quantity supplied is Q_2. Similarly, we have demand curves at D_3 and D_4 and corresponding supplies are Q_3 and Q_4. The firm's marginal cost curve which gives the marginal cost corresponding to each level of output is nothing but firm's supply curve that gives fee quantity the firm will supply at each price.

For prices below AVC, the firm will supply zero units because here the firm is unable to meet even its variable cost for prices above AVC the firm will equate price and marginal cost.

When price is just meeting the AVC, the firm will break-even (Rs. 2 here). Here it is just meeting its average variable costs and there are no profits or losses.

Thus in perfect competition the firm's marginal cost curve above AVC has the identical shape of the firm's supply curve.

Equilibrium of the firm in the Short Run :

In the short run, a firm will attain equilibrium position and at the same time it will earn supernormal profits, normal profits or losses depending upon its cost conditions.

Supernormal Profits:

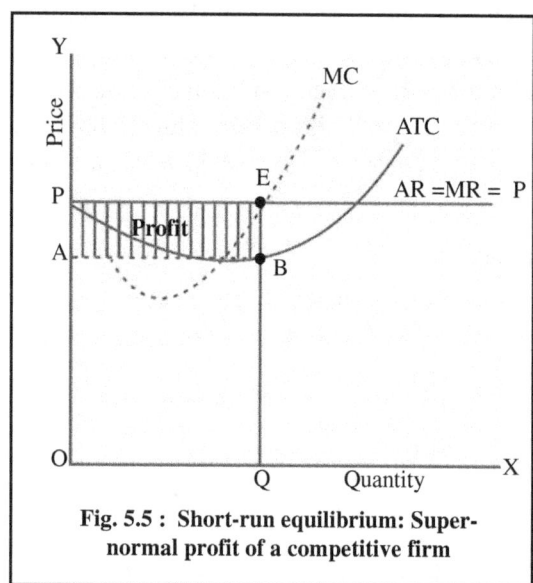

Fig. 5.5 : Short-run equilibrium: Super-normal profit of a competitive firm

There is a difference between normal profits and supernormal profits. When the average revenue of a firm is just equal to its average total cost, it earns normal profits. It is to be noted here that a normal percentage of profits for the entrepreneur for his managerial services is already included in the cost of production. When a firm earns supernormal profits its average revenues are more than its average total cost. Thus, in additional to normal rate of profit, the firm earns additional profits.

The figure 5.5 shows how a firm can earn supernormal profit in the short run.

The diagram shows that in order to attain equilibrium, the firm tries to equate marginal revenue with marginal cost. MR (marginal revenue) curve is a horizontal line and MC (marginal cost) curve is a U-shaped curve which cuts the MR curve at E. At E, MR=MC. OQ is the equilibrium output for the firm. The firm's profit per unit is EB (AR-ATC), AR is EB and ATC is BQ. Total profits are ABEP.

Normal profits:

When the firm just meets its average total cost, it earns normal profits. Here AR=ATC.

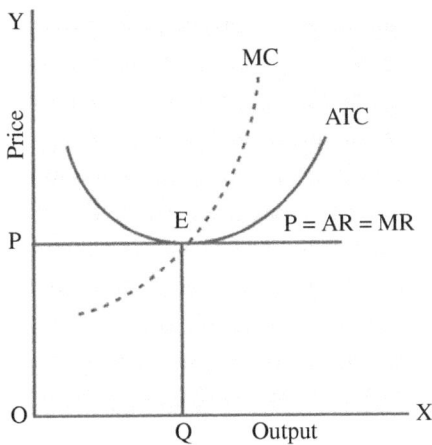

Fig. 5.6 : Short-run equilibrium of a competitive firm : Normal Profits

The figure shows that MR=MC at E. The equilibrium output is OQ. Since here AR=ATC or OP=EQ, the firm is just earning normal profits.

Losses :

The firm can be in a equilibrium position and still makes losses. This is the position when the firm is minimising losses. When the firm is able to meet its variable cost and a part of fixed cost it will try to continue production in the short run. If it recovers a part of the fixed cost, it will be beneficial for it to continue production because fixed costs such as costs towards plant and machinery, building etc. are already incurred and in such a case it will be able to recover part of it. But if a firm is unable to meet its average variable cost also, it will better for it to shut down.

In figure 5.7, E is the equilibrium point and at this point AR=EQ and AC=BQ since BQ > EQ, firm is earning BE per unit loss and total loss is ABEP.

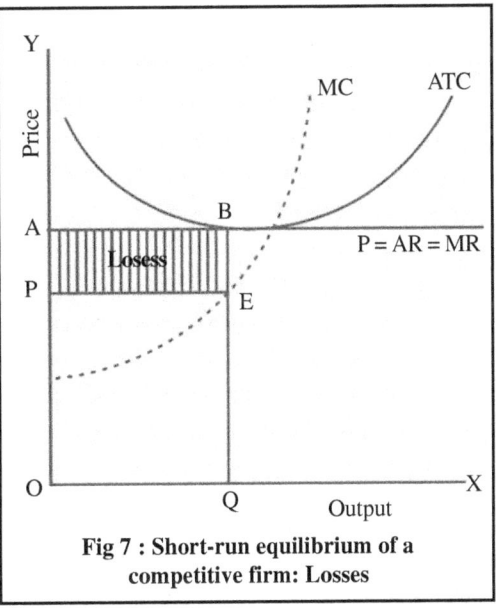

Fig 7 : Short-run equilibrium of a competitive firm: Losses

Long-Run Equilibrium of the Firm:

In the long run firms are in equilibrium when they have adjusted their plant so as to produce at the minimum point of their long run AC curve, which is tangent to the demand curve defined by the market price. In the long run the firms will be earning just normal profits, which are included in the AC. If they make supernormal profits new firms will be attracted in the industry; this will lead to a fall in price (a down ward shift in the individual demand curves) and an upward shift of the cost curves due to the increase of the prices of factors as the industry expands. These changes will continue until the AC is tangent to the demand curve. If the firms make losses in the short run they will leave the industry in the long run. This will raise the price and costs may fall as the industry contracts, until the remaining firms in the industry cover their total costs inclusive of the normal rate of profit. In fig.5.8 we show how firms adjust to their long-run equilibrium position. If the price is OP, the firm is making super-normal profits working with the plant whose cost is denoted by SAC_1. It will, therefore, have an incentive to build new capacity and it will move along its LAC. At the same time new firms will be entering the industry attracted by the excess profits. As the quantity supplied in the market increases, the supply curve in the market will shift to the right and price will fall until it reaches the level of OP_1 (in figure 5.8a) at which the firms and the industry are in long run equilibrium.

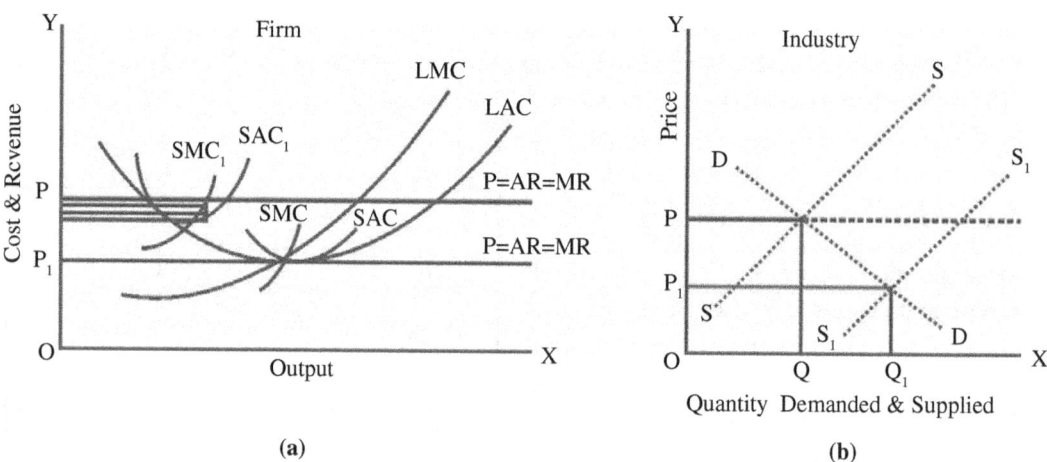

Fig. 5.8 : Long-run equilitrium of the firm in a pertectly competitive market

The condition for the long-run equilibrium of the firm is that the marginal cost be equal to the price and the long-run average cost

i.e. $$LMC = LAC = P$$

The firm adjusts its plant size so as to produce that level of output at which the LAC is the minimum possible. At equilibrium the short run marginal cost is equal to the long-run marginal cost and the short-run average cost is equal to the long-run average cost. Thus in the long-run we have,

$$SMC = LMC = SAC = LAC = P = MR$$

This implies that at the minimum point of the LAC the corresponding (short-run) plant is worked at its optimal capacity, so that the minima of the LAC and SAC coincide. On the other hand, the LMC cuts the LAC at its minimum point and the SMC cuts the SAC at its minimum point. Thus at the minimum point of the LAC the above equality is achieved.

Long-run equilibrium of the industry : When

(i) all the firms are earning normal profits only i.e. all the firms are in equilibrium

(ii) there is no further entry or exit from the market, the industry is said to have attained long-run equilibrium.

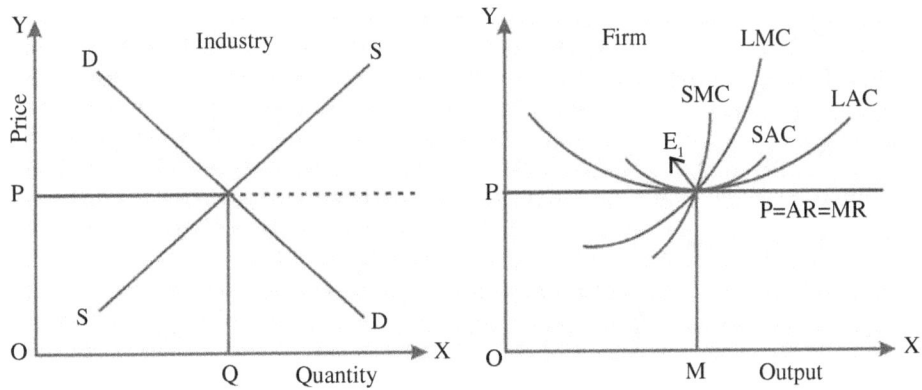

Fig. 5.9 : Long-run equilitrium of a competitive indusitry and its firms

Fig. 5.9 shows that in the long-run AR =MR =LAC =LMC at E_1 Since E_1 is the minimum point of LAC curve, the firm produces equilibrium output OM at the minimum (optimum) cost. The firm producing output at optimum cost is called an optimum firm. All the firms in the perfect competition in long-run are optimum firms having optimum size and these firms charge minimum possible price which just covers their marginal cost.

Thus in the long-run

(i)   LAR = LMR = P = LMC = LAC

(ii)   the firms just earn normal profits

(iii) Competitive firms are of optimum size.

Thus we notice that in perfect competition the market mechanism leads to an optimal allocation of resources in the long run. But it should be remembered that the perfectly competitive market system is a myth. This is because the assumptions on which this system is based are never found in the real world market conditions.

5. 3 MONOPOLY

The term monopoly refers to that market in which there is a single seller of goods which has no *close substitute*. Pure monopoly is never found in practice. However, in public utilities such as transport, water and electricity, we generally find monopoly form of market.

Features of Monopoly Market :

The following are the major features of the monopoly market:

1) *Single seller of the product :* In a monopoly market there is only one firm producing or supplying a product. This single firm constitutes the industry and as such there is no

distinction between the firm and the industry in a monopoly market.

2) *Restrictions to Entry :* In a monopoly market, there are strong barriers to entry. The barriers to entry could be economic, institutional, legal or artificial.

3) *No close-substitutes :* The monopolist generally sells a product which has no close substitutes. In such a case, the cross elasticity of demand for the monopolist's product and any other product is zero or very small. The price elasticity of demand for monopolist's product is also less than one. As a result, the monopolist faces a downward sloping demand curve.

4) *Monopolist are price maker :* A monopolist firm is a price maker. The monopolist determines the price as well as output for his product

Sources of monopoly power :

There may be different reasons for the emergence of monopoly power. These are factors which restrict the entryof new firms in the monopoly market. Some of these factors are as follows:

1) *Immobility of factors of production :* Such immobility means that existing suppliers cannot be challenged by new entrants. It may arise through:

   (a) Legal prohibition of new entrants as with public utilities, where many firms would create technical difficulties, e.g. gas, electricity, water and telephone services.

   (b) Patents, copyrights and trademarks, where the object is to promote inventions and development of new ideas.

   (c) Government policy of establishing single buying and selling agencies e.g. marketing boards.

   (d) Control of the source of supply by one firm, e.g. minerals, specialist workers, trade unions and professional associations.

2) *Ignorance :* A monopoly may persist largely through the ignorance of possible competitors. They may not know about the super-normal profits being made by the existing firm, or they may be unable to acquire the necessary know-how, e.g. for involved technical processes.

3) *Indivisibilities :* Whereas the original firm may have been able to build up its size gradually, new firms may find it difficult to raise the large capital required to produce on a scale which is cost-competitive, e.g. with cars, drugs, computers.

   In some cases, too, the efficient scale of plant may be so large relative to the market that there is scope for only one firm. This applies to many of the public utilities, e.g. transport, water, electricity generation, etc.

4) A deliberate policy of excluding competitors : There can also be a deliberate action to exclude competitors. Firms producing or selling the same good may combine, or a competitor may be subject to a takeover bid. This will give monopoly powers to the firms who have joined together to form an association.

Monopolist's Revenue Curves :

Since the monopolist firm is assumed to be the only producer of a particular product, its demand curve is identical with the market demand curve for the product. The market demand curve, which exhibits the total quantity of a product that buyers will offer to buy at each price, also shows the quantity that the monopolist will be able to sell at every price that he sets. If we assume that the monopolist sets a single price and supplies all buyers who wish to purchase at that price, we can easily find his average revenue and marginal revenue curves.

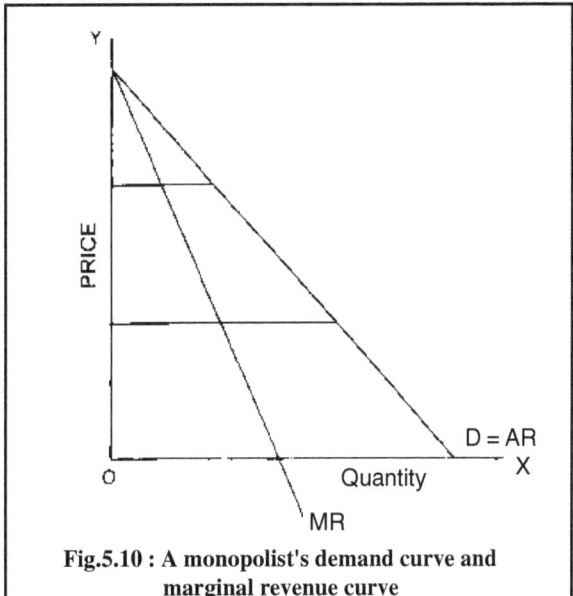

Fig.5.10 : A monopolist's demand curve and marginal revenue curve

Suppose the straight line in Fig.5.10 is the market demand for a particular product 'A'. Suppose Mr. X and Co. is the single producer of the product A so that it faces the entire market demand and hence the down-ward sloping demand curve.

Table: Average revenue, total revenue and marginal revenue for a monopolist (selected value of demand curve)

Quantity sold	Average Revenue P = AR	Total Revenue (TR)	Marginal Revenue (MR)
0	10.00	0	
1	9.50	9.50	9.50
2	9.00	18.00	8.50
3	8.50	25.50	7.50
4	8.00	32.00	6.50
5	7.50	37.50	5.50
6	7.00	42.00	4.50
7	6.50	45.50	3.50
8	6.00	48.00	2.50
9	5.50	49.50	1.50
10	5.00	50.00	.50
11	4.50	49.50	(-).50

It is clear from the above table and graph that if the seller wishes to charge Rs. 10, he cannot sell any unit. If he wants to sell, he has to decrease the price for each additional unit of the commodity. Because the seller charges a single price for all units he sells, average revenue per unit is identical with price, and thus the market demand curve is the average revenue for the monopolist.

In perfect competition, average and marginal revenue are identical, but this is not the case in a monopoly since the monopoly knows that if he wishes to increase his sales he will have to reduce the price of the product.

On the basis of above table and graph, the relationship between AR and MR of a monopoly firm can be stated as follows:

(i)   AR and MR are both negative sloped (downward sloping) curves.

(ii)   MR curve lies between the AR curve and price axis i.e. the Y axis. and

(iii) AR cannot be zero, but MR can be zero or even negative.

Relationship between Marginal Revenue, Average Revenue, Total Revenue and Elasticity of Demand: It is to be noted that marginal revenue, average revenue and price elasticity of demand are uniquely related to one another through the formula:

$$MR = AR \times \frac{e-1}{e}$$

Where   e = price elasticity of demand

Thus   If e = 1, MR = AR = $0 \times \frac{1-1}{1} = 0$

If e > 1, MR will be positive and

If e < 1, MR will be negative

In a straight line demand curve, we know that the elasticity of the middle point is equal to one. If follows that marginal revenue corresponding to the middle point of the demand curve (or AR curve) will be zero.

Consider Fig.5.11 C is the middle point of the Average Revenue (AR) Curve. At point C, elasticity is equal to one. Corresponding to C, marginal revenue will be zero. Thus MR is shown to be cutting X-axis in fig. (i) at point N which corresponds to point C on the AR Curve. Since MR is zero here, total revenue will be maximum. This is shown in fig.(ii) where TR reaches H-the highest point. At a greater quantity than ON, elasticity of the AR curve is less than one and the marginal revenue is negative. Marginal revenue being negative beyond ON means that total revenue will diminish if a quantity larger than ON is sold. Thus TR curve is shown to be falling after reaching H point. At a lower quantity than ON, elasticity of the AR curve is greater than one and the marginal revenue is positive. Marginal revenue being positive before ON means that total revenue will increase with increase in the quantity. This is shown by rising portion of TR curve upto point ON, where it is highest.

In brief we can say that

(i)   when e > 1, total revenue is rising and marginal revenue is positive,

(ii) when e = 1, total revenue is maximum and marginal revenue is zero, and

(iii) When e < 1, total revenue is falling, and marginal revenue is negative.

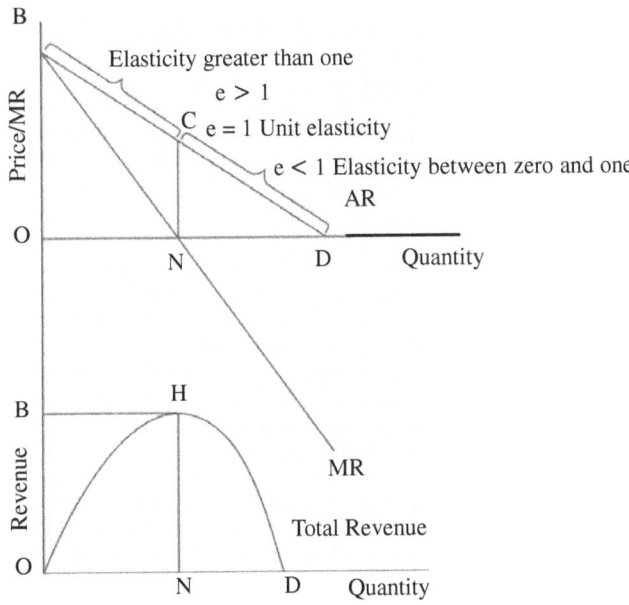

Fig 5.11: The relation of total, average, marginal revenue to elasticity of demand

Having known the above relationship we can easily say that a profit maximising monopolist will never choose to sell an output for which demand is inelastic (e) because here his total revenue will fall and marginal revenue will be negative. In other words, it will not be profitable for him to produce beyond the middle point on the demand curve because he can always increase his revenue by reducing output. This will reduce his cost as well.

Short-run Equilibrium of Monopoly

Conditions for the equilibrium: The twin conditions for equilibrium in a monopoly market are same as discussed earlier.

(i) MC = MR

(ii) MC curve must cut MR curve from below graphically, we can depict these conditions in figure 5.12

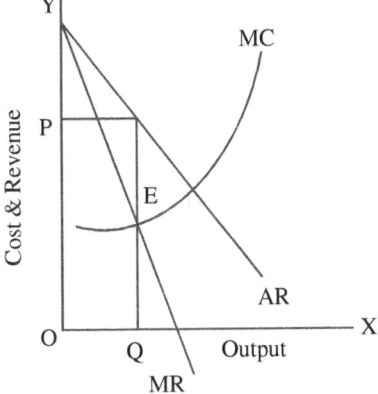

Fig. 5.12 : Equilibrium Position of a monopolist (Short-run)

The figure shows that MC curve cuts MR curve at E. That means at E, equilibrium price is OP and equilibrium output is OQ.

In order to know whether the monopolist is making profits or losses in the short run, we need to introduce average total cost curve. The following figure shows how the firm makes profits in the short run.

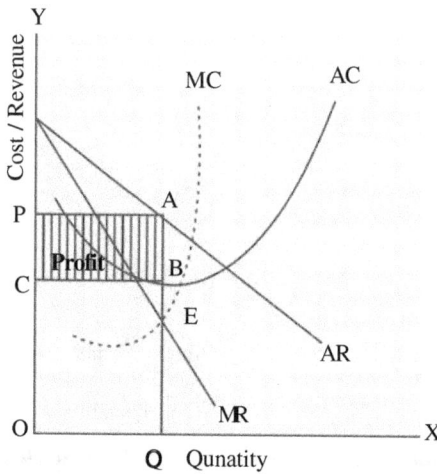

Fig.5.13: Firm's equilibrium under monopoly: maximisation of profits

Figure 5.13 shows that MC cuts MR at E to give equilibrium output as OQ. At OQ, price charged is OP (we find this by extending line EQ till it touches AR or demand curve). Also at OQ, the cost per unit is BQ. Therefore, profit per unit is AB or total profit is ABCP.

Can a monopolist incur losses?

One of the misconceptions about a monopolist is that he always makes profits. Nothing guarantees that a monopolist makes profits. It all depends upon his demand and cost conditions. If he faces a very low demand for his product and his cost conditions are such that ATC > AR, he will not be making profits but incurs losses. Figure 5.14 depicts this position.

In the figure 5.14 MC cuts MR at E. Here E is the point of loss minimisation. At E, equilibrium output is OQ and equilibrium price is OP. Cost corresponding to OQ is QA. Cost per unit of output i.e. QA is greater than revenue per unit which is BQ. Thus the monopolist incurs losses to the extent of AB

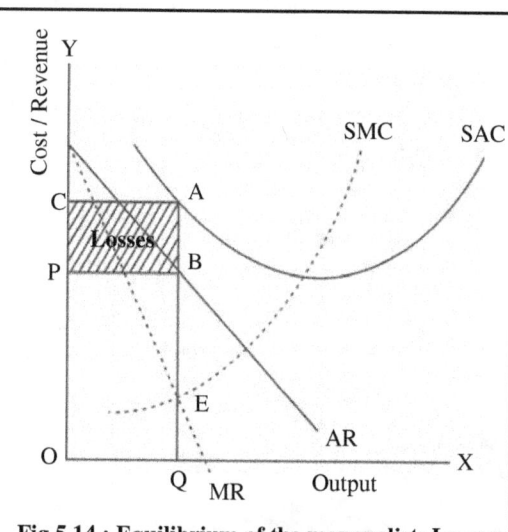

Fig.5.14 : Equilibrium of the monopolist: Losses in the short run

per unit or total loss is ABPC. Whether the monopolist stays in business in the short run depends upon whether he meets his average variable cost or not. If he covers average variable cost and at least a part of fixed cost, he will not shut down because he contributes something towards fixed costs which are already incurred. If he is unable to meet his average variable cost even, he will shut down.

Long Run Equilibrium :

Long-run is a period long enough to allow the monopolist to adjust his plant size or use his existing plant at any level that maximises his profit. In the absence of competition, the monopolist need not produce at the optimal level. He can produce at sub-optimal scale also. In other words, he need not reach the minimum of LAC curve, he can stop at any place where his profits are maximum.

However, one thing is certain: The monopolist will not continue if he makes losses in the long-run. He will continue to make super-normal profits even in the long-run as entry of outside firms is blocked.

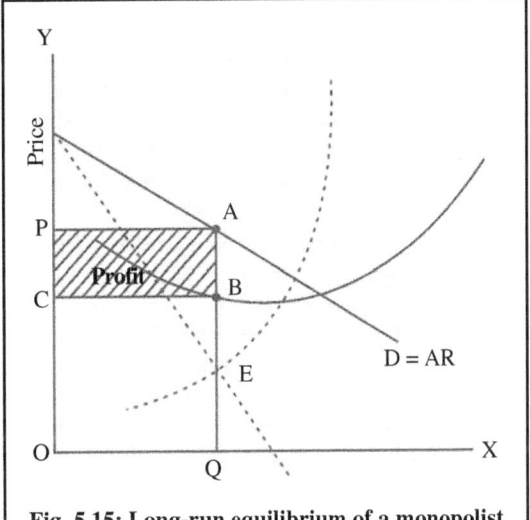

Fig. 5.15: Long-run equilibrium of a monopolist

Price Discrimination :

Price discrimination cannot persist under perfect competition because the seller has no influence over market determined rate. Price discrimination requires an element of monopoly so that the seller can influence the price of his product. Price discrimination occurs when a producer sells a specific commodity or service to different buyers at two or more different prices for reasons not associated with differences in cost.

Conditions for price discrimination :

Price discrimination is possible only under the following conditions:
1) *Monopoly Power :* The seller should have some control over the supply of his product i.e. monopoly power in some form is necessary to (not sufficient) discriminate price.
2) *Existence of two or more sub-markets :* The seller should be able to divide his market into two or more sub-markets.
3) *Existence of different price elasticity of demand in different sub-markets :* The price-elasticity of the product should be different in different markets. The monopolist fixes up a high price for his product for those buyers whose price elasticity of demand for the product is less than one. This implies that when the monopolist charges a higher price from them, they do not significantly reduce their purchases in response to high price.

4) *Effective separation of the sub-markets :* It should not be possible for the buyers of low priced market to resell the product to the buyers of high-priced market.

Consider the following examples.

(a) Doctors are able to separate patients with high income from those with low income and charge higher fee from the former.

(b) Railway separate high-value or relatively small-bulk commodities which can bear higher freight charges from other categories of goods.

(c) Some countries dump goods at low prices in foreign markets to capture them.

(d) Some universities charge higher tuition fees from evening class students than from other scholars.

(e) A lower subscription is charged from student readers in case of certain journals.

Price - output determination under price discrimination :

Suppose there are two markets to which a price-discriminating monopolist has to sell his product-market A and market B. Both markets have different price elasticities-demand is more elastic in market B than in market A. This is shown in figure 5.16:

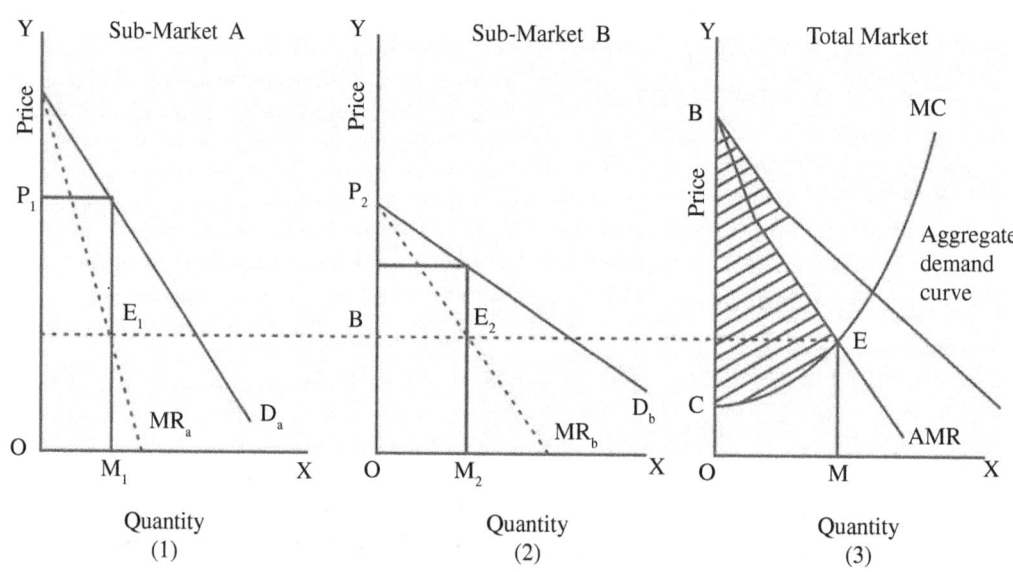

Fig. 5.16 : Fixation of total output and different prices in the two markets A and B by the discriminating monopolist

The figure shows D_a and D_b as the average revenue curves for the respective markets. MR_a and MR_b are the corresponding marginal revenue curves. Since all his output is under one organisation, there is only one marginal cost curve. AMR is the total marginal revenue curve. It is a lateral summation of the two curves-MR_a and MR_b.

Conditions for equilibrium :

(i) The discriminating monopolist is guided by the same rule as any other producer for maximising his profits. He equates MC with AMR (aggregate marginal revenue). Thus condition one is MC = AMR.

(ii) The discriminating monopolist has not only to decide how much to produce but has to distribute the output in two sub- markets in such a way and at such a price, that he maximises his profits. The profit in each market is maximised by equating MC to the corresponding MR of each market i.e. $MC = MR_a = MR_b$

In fig. 5.16, we see that MC and AMR intersect at point E and OM is therefore total output of the monopolist, Ihe line EM is the line of equal marginal revenue. It indicates that OM_1 will be sold in market A at the price P_1M_1 and OM_2 is sold in market B at the price P_2M_2. Under this arrangement, the marginal cost of the total output EM is equal to marginal revenue in each separate market.

The discriminating monpolist charges a higher price from the market which has a relatively inelastic demand. The market which is highly responsive is charged less. On the whole, the monopolist benefits from both the markets.

5.4 IMPERFECT COMPETITION-MONOPOLISTIC COMPETITION

In real world neither perfect competition nor monopoly markets are found. In fact most of the markets have the characteristics of monopolistic market structure.

Consider the market for soaps and detergents. Among the well known brands on sale are Lux, Liril, Pears, Lifebuoy Plus, Dove and so many others. The market for soaps seems to be an example of perfect competition since all the soaps are almost similar. But on a close inspection we find that each seller has at least some variatioin between his product and those of his competitors. For example, where as Lux is exhibited to be a beauty soap, Liril is more associated with freshness.The area of product and service differentiation gives each seller a chance to attract business to himself on some basis other than price.This is the monopolistic part of market situation. Thus this market contains features of both the markets discussed earlier - monopoly and perfect competition. In fact, this type of market is more common that pure competition or pure monopoly. The industries in monopolistic competition include clothing manufacturing and retail trade in large cities.

Features of monopolistic competition :

1) *Large number of sellers :* In a monopolistically competitive market, there are a large number of sellers who individually have a small share in the market.

2) *Product differentiation:* In a monopolistic competitive market, the products of different sellers are differentiated on the basis of brands. These brands are generally so much

advertised that a consumer starts associating the brand with a particular manufacturer and a type of brand loyalty is developed. Product differentiation gives rise to an element of monopoly to the producer over the competing product. As such, the producer of an individual brand can raise the price of his product knowing that he will not lose all the customers to other brands because of absence of perfect substitutability. Since, however, all the brands are close substitutes of one another, the seller will lose some of his customers to his competitors. Thus this market is a blend of monopoly and perfect competition.

3) *Free entry and exit :* New firms are free to enter into the market and existing firms are free to quit it.

4) *Non-price competition :* In a monopolistically competitive market, sellers try to compete on basis other than price, as for example aggressive advertising, product development, better distribution arrangements, efficient after-sales service, and so on. A key base of non-price competition is a deliberate policy of product differentiation. Sellers attempt to promote their products not by cutting prices but by incurring high expenditure on publicity and advertisement and other sale promoting techniques mentioned above. This is because price competition may result in price - wars which may throw a few firms out of market.

Price-output determination under monopolistic competition : Equilibrium of a firm : In a monopolistically competitive market since the product is differentiated between firms, each firm does not face a perfectly elastic demand for its products. Each firm is a price maker and is in a position to determine price of its own product. As such, the firm is faced with a downward sloping demand curve for its product. Generally, the less differentiated the product is from its competitors, the more elastic this curve will be.

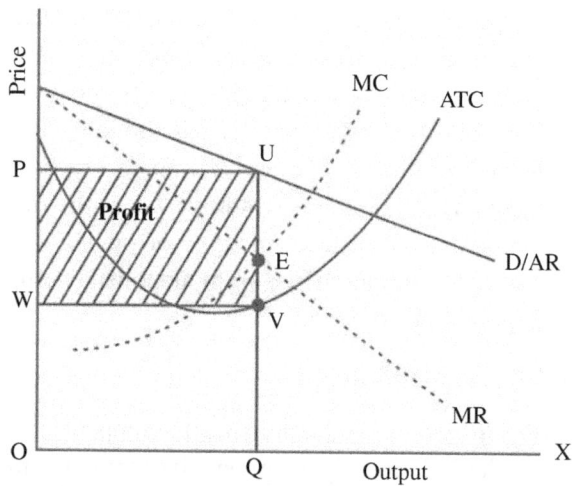

Fig. 5.17: Short-run equilibrium of a firm in monopolistic competition: Super-normal profits

The firm depicted in figure 5.17 has a down-ward sloping but flat demand curve for its product. The firm is assumed to have U shaped short-run cost curve.

Conditions for the Equilibrium of an individual firm :

The conditions for price-output determination and equilibrium of an individual firm may be stated as follows:

(i)　MC = MR

(ii)　MC curve must cut MR curve from below

Figure 5.17 shows that MC cuts MR curve at E. At E, the equilibrium price is OP and equilibrium output is OQ. Since per unit cost is QV, per unit super-normal profit (i.e. price-cost) is UV (or PW) and total super-normal profit is PUVW.

Losses :

The firm may also be earning losses in the short-run. This is shown in fig.5.18.

The figure shows that per unit cost (QV) is higher than price OP (or QU) of the product of the firm and loss per unit is UV (QV- QU). Total loss is PUVW.

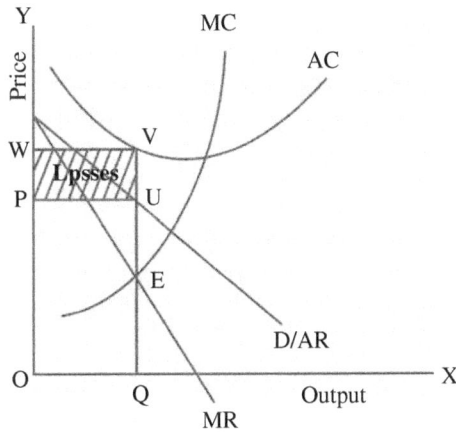

Fig. 5.18 : Short-run equilibrium of a firm in Monopolistic Competition - With losses

Long –Run Equilibrium of the firm :

If the firms in a monopolistically competitive industry earn super-normal profits in the short-run, there will be an incentive for new firms to enter the industry. As more firms enter, profits per firm will go on decreasing as the total demand for the product will be shared among a larger number of firms. This will happen till all the profits are wiped away and all the firms earn only normal profits. Thus in the long-run all the firms will earn only normal profits.

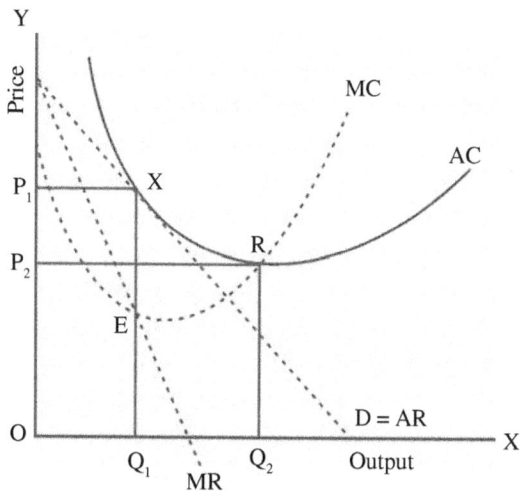

Fig. 5. 19 : The long-term equilibrium of a firm in monopolistic competition

Figure 5.19 shows the long-run equilibrium of *a* firm in *a* monopolistically competitive market. The average revenue curve touches the average cost curve at point X corresponding to quantity Q_1 and price P_1 At equilibrium (i.e. MC=MR) profits are zero, since average revenue equals average costs. All firms are earning zero super normal profits or just normal profits.

In case of losses in the short-run, the loss making firms will exit from the market and, this will go on till the remaining firms make normal profits only.

An individual firm in the long-run is in equilibrium position at a position where it has excess capacity. That is, it is producing a lower quantity than its full capacity level. The firm in Figure 5.19, could expand its output from Q_1 to Q_2 and reduce average costs. But it does not do so because to do so would be to reduce average revenue even more than average costs. It would have to reduce price to P_2 to gain extra sales and avoid losses. It implies that firms in monopolistic competition are not of optimum size and there exists excess capacity of production with each firm.

5.5 OLIGOPOLY

Oligopoly is an important form of imperfect competition. Oligopoly is often described as 'competition among the few'. In other words, when there are few (two to ten) sellers in a market selling homogeneous or differentiated products, oligopoly is said to exist. Consider the example of cold drinks industry or automobile industry. There are a handful firms manufacturing cold drinks in India. Similarly there are a few members of automobile industry in India.

Features of Oligopoly Market:

1) *Interdependence :* The most important feature of oligopoly is interdependence in decision-making of the few firms which comprise the industry. This is because when the number of competitors is few, any change in price, output, product, by a firm will have direct

effect on the competitors, who will then change their own prices, output or advertising technique as the case may be. It is, therefore, clear that an oligopolistic firm must consider not only the market demand for the industry product but also the reactions of other firms in the industry to any major decision it takes.

2) *Importance of advertising and selling costs :* A direct effect of interdependence of oligopolists is that the various firms have to employ various aggressive and defensive marketing weapons to gain a greater share in the market or to maintain their share. For this various firms have to incur a good deal of costs on advertising and other measures of sales promotion. Therefore, there is a great importance of advertising and selling costs in an oligopoly market. Firms in such type of market avoid price cutting and try to compete on non-price basis because if they start under cutting one another a type of price-war will emerge which will drive a few of them out of the market as customers will try to buy from the seller selling at the cheapest price.

3) *Group behaviour :* The theory of oligopoly is a theory of group behaviour, not of mass or individual behaviour and to assume profit maximising behaviour on oligopolist's part may not be very valid. There is no generally accepted theory of group behaviour. Each oligopolist closely watches the business behaviour of the other oligopolists in the industry and designs his moves on the basis of some assumptions of how they behave or likely to behave.

Price and output decisions in an oligopolistic market :

Because of interdependence an oligopolistic firm cannot assume that its rival firms will keep their prices and quantities constant, when it makes changes in its price and/or quantity. When an oligopolistic firm changes its price, its rival firms will retaliate or react and change their prices which in turn would affect the demand of the former firm. Therefore, an oligopolistic firm cannot have sure and definite demand curve, since it keeps shifting as the rivals change their prices in reaction to the price changes made by it. Now when an oligopolist does not know his demand curve, what price and output he will fix cannot be ascertained by economic analysis. However, economists have established a number of price-output models for oligopoly market depending upon the behaviour pattern of the members of the group.

Since a wide variety of behaviour patterns becomes possible, a large variety of models depending upon different assumptions about the behaviour of the oligopolistic group have been evolved. A few important are as follows :

1) Some economists have assumed that oligopolist firms ignore interdependence. Now, when interdependence disappears from decision-making of the oligopolistic firms, the demand curve facing the oligopolist becomes determinate and can be ascertained. Once the demand curve becomes determinate, we can easily find the equilibrium price and output of a particular oligopolist firm by equating its marginal revenue with its marginal cost.

2) Another approach is to provide a determinate solution to the price and output problem of oligopoly is to assume that an oligopolist is able to predict the reaction pattern and

counter moves of his rivals. In this connection various oligopoly models based on different assumptions regarding the particular reaction pattern of the rivals have been propounded. Famous among these are Cournot's model, Chamberline model and Sweezy model.

3) Another approach to oligopoly problem assumes that oligopoly firms realising their interdependence will pursue their common interest and will form a collusion, formal or tacit, that is they will enter into an agreement and work in the pursuit of their common interests. They will jointly act as a monopolist firm and fix their price in such a way their joint profits are maximum. They will then share the profits, market or output as agreed between them. OPEC (Organisation of Petroleum Exporting Countries) is the best example of such type of agreement among oligopolists.

Thus, we find that fixing of price under oligopoly market situation is very difficult and involves a number of assumptions.

Kinked Demand Curve :

It has been observed that in many oligopolistic industries prices remain sticky or inflexible for a long time. They tend to change infrequently, even in the face of declining costs. Many explanations have been given for this price rigidity under oligopoly and the most popular explanation is kinked demand curve hypothesis given by an American economist Sweezy.

The demand curve facing an oligopolist, according to the kinked demand curve hypothesis, has a 'kink' at the level of the prevailing price. The kink is formed at the prevailing price level. It is because the segment of the demand curve above the prevailing price level is highly elastic and the segment of the demand curve below the prevailing price level is inelastic. A kinked demand curve dD with a kink at point P has been shown in Fig. 5.20.

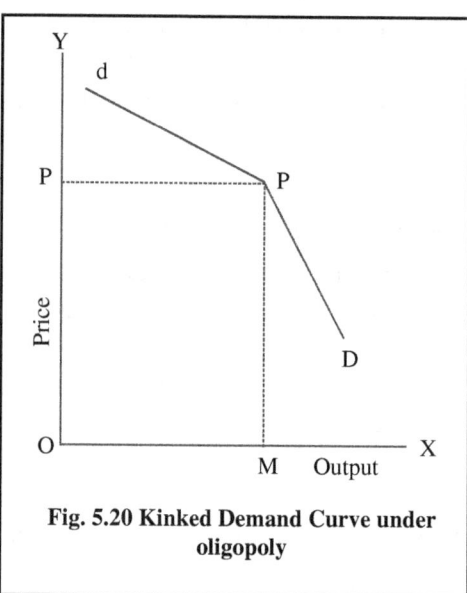

Fig. 5.20 Kinked Demand Curve under oligopoly

The prevailing price level is MP and the firm produces and sells output OM. Now the upper segment dP of the demand curve dD is relatively elastic and lower segment PD is relatively inelastic. This difference in elasticities is due to the particular competitive reaction pattern assumed by the kinky demand curve hypothesis. This assumed pattern is:

Each oligopolist believes that if he lowers the price below the prevailing level its competitors will follow him and will accordingly lower prices, whereas if he raises the price above the prevailing level, its competitors will not follow its increase in price.

This is because when an oligopolist lowers the price of its product its competitors will feel that if they do not follow the price cut their customers will run away and buy from the firm which has lowered the price. Thus in order to maintain their customers they will also lower their prices. Thus the upper portion of the demand curve is price elastic. On the other hand, if a firm increases the price of its product there will a substantial reduction in its sales because as a result of the rise in its price, its customers will withdraw from it and go to its competitors which will welcome the new customers and will gain in sales. These happy competitors will have therefore no motivation to match the price rise. The oligopolist who raises its price will lose a great deal and will therefore refrain from increasing price. This behaviour of the oligopolists explain the inelastic lower portion of the demand curve.

Each oligopolist will, thus, adhere to the prevailing price seeing no gain in changing it and a kink will be formed at the prevailing price. Thus, rigid or sticky prices are explained according to the kinked demand curve theory.

The features of the various types of market forms are summarised in the table given below:

Classification of Market Forms

Form of Market Structure	Number of firms	Nature of product	Price Elasticity of Demand of a firm	Degree of Control over price
(a) Perfect competition	A large number of firms	Homogeneous	Infinite	None
(b) Monopoly	One	Unique product without close substitute	Small	Very Conside rable
(c) Imperfect Competition				
(i) Monopolistic Competition	A large number of firms	Differentiated products	Large	Some
(ii) Oligopoly	Few Firms	Homogeneous or differentiated product	Small	Some

Perfect Competition is said to prevail where there is a large number of firms producing a homogeneous product. No individual firm is in a position to influence the price of the product and therefore the demand curve facing it will be a horizontal straight line at the prevailing market price. Short-run equilibrium price of the firm is at a point where MC=MR of the firm. In the short-run firms may be earning super normal profits and some firms may be earning losses at the equilibrium price. In the long-run all the supernormal profits or losses' get wiped away with entry or exit of the firms the industry and all the firms earn normal profits.

Monopoly is an extreme form of imperfect competition with a single seller of a product which has no close substitutes. As such, a monopolist has considerable control over the price of his product. Short-run equilibrium of the monopolist is at a point where MC=MR. In the long run he may continue to have super normal profits.

Monopoly control over the product gives rise to price- discrimination (i.e. charging different prices for the same product from different consumers).

Imperfect Competition is an important category wherein the individual firm exercises control over the price to a smaller or larger degree depending upon the degree of imperfection present.

Monopolistic competition. In this type of market, there are a large number of monopolists competing with one another. Demand curve is highly elastic and a firm enjoys come control over the price.

Oligopoly in which there is competition among the few firms producing homogeneous or differentiated products. The limited number of firms ensures that each of them will have to consider the group reaction to any action it takes.

Exercise

1) What are the features of a perfectly competitive market?
2) Explain price determination both in short-run and long-run under
   (a) Perfect Competition
   (b) Monopoly
3) What is price discrimination? How does a discriminating monopolist maximise profits?
4) What are the characteristics of an oligopoly market? How are price and quantity determined under such a market?
5) What is kinked demand curve hypothesis?
6) What are the characteristics of a monopolistically competitive market? Why do firms under such a market have excess capacity even in the long-run?
7) Distinguishm between perfect competition, monopolistic competition, oligopoly and Monopoly.

Factor Pricing

Contents

6.1 MARGINAL PRODUCTIVITY THEORY OF DISTRIBUTION

The marginal productivity theory of distribution is also known as the General Theory of Distribution. It has been propounded by J. B. Clark. Jevons, Marshall and Hicks have made important contributions to the development of this theory. The theory provides a general explanation of how the income of each factor of production is determined.

The factors of production, namely land, labour, capital and enterprise provide their productive service or participate in production activity and create national wealth. This national wealth in turn is distributed among the factors of production in the form of rent, wages, interest and profit as a remuneration for their contribution to production activity. Thus distribution means the sharing of the wealth that is produced among the different factors of production.

The theory states that the price of factor of production is governed by its marginal productivity. The theory analyses- the process of equilibrium in the factor market under perfect competitive conditions. When there is perfect competition in the factor market, the firm can employ any number of factor units at the prevailing market price. The firm will be in equilibrium at that point where the marginal productivity of the factors is equal to its price. Hence the price or return of the factor equals its marginal productivity.

Meaning of marginal productivity: To understand the theory, the various concepts of marginal productivity should be cleared.

i) *Marginal Physical Productivity (MPP)* : It refers to the addition made'to the total physical product by employing one more unit of a factor, the quality of other factors\ remaining the constant. If 10 workers produce 60 units of a commodity and when 11 workers are employed, they produce 70 units of that commodity. One more workers is employed and the production goes upto 70 units so here marginal physical productivity is 10 units. (70-60 units)

ii) *Marginal Value Product (MVP)* : When MPP is multiplied by price, we get MVP. It is the monetary representation of marginal physical productivity.

$$MVP = MPP \times Price$$

in the example,

eleventh worker has produced 10 units of a commodity. If the price of per unit of commodity is Rs. 15 the MVP = Rs. 15 × 10 = Rs. 150.

iii) *Marginal Revenue Productivity (MRP)* : It is addition made to total revenue by employing an additional unit of factor, quantity of other factors remaining constant.

$$MRP = MPP \times MR$$

If 10 workers produce Units worth Rs. 1000 and 11 workers produce units worth. Rs. 1100, the MRP = Rs. 1100 - Rs. 1000 = Rs. 100. Under perfect competition price = Average Revenue (AR) and marginal Revenue (MR). So MRP and MVP are one and the same thing. But in case of imperfect competition, MR is always less than price or AR, Hence MRP will not be equal to MVP. MVP will be less than MRP.

iv) *Average Revenue Productivity (ARP)* : It is the average revenue per unit of a factor of production. If total revenue productivity its divided by total production. We get average revenue productivity.

Relation between ARP and MRR: The relation between ARP and MRP is similar to the relation between average cost and marginal cost. The only difference is that AC and MC are U shaped while ARP and MRP are having the shape of reverse U that is n as shown in following diagram" :

With increase in production, productive efficiency oftahe factors increase and so the

ARP and MRP are rising but beyond a certain\ point both of them start falling. MRP is lies below ARP. This is shown in diagram. Diagram shows that upto point E. ARP and MRP are rising and MRP lies above ARP. At point E both are Equal. But after the point, both ARP and MRP start falling. Beyond point E. MRP is below ARP.

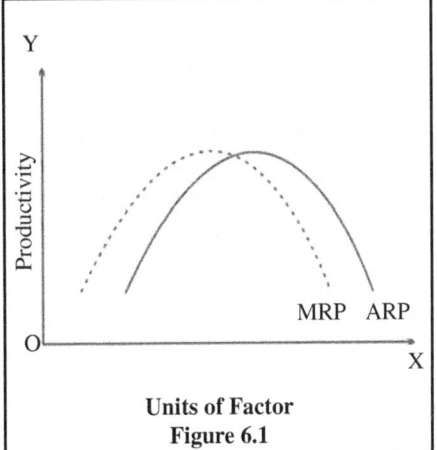

Units of Factor
Figure 6.1

Assumption of the theory

The marginal productivity theory holds good only on the following assumptions.

i) The theory holds good only if there is *perfect competition* in the product as well as in the factor market.

ii) That all the factor units are *identical* is assumed.

iii) Factor units are perfectly *substitute* for one another.

iv) It is assumed that factors are *"perfectly mobile"*.

v) The factors are *perfectly divisible.*

vi) The supply of factors are *elastic.*

vii) The theory is based on the assumption of *'full Employment'*

viii) The theory holds good in the *long* run,

Marginal productivity theory explains the following points.

i) Reward of each factor unit will be equal to its marginal productivity : Rational producer aims either at maximising his profit or minimising his losses. For this, every producer compares the price paid to the factors with its productivity. The price paid to the factor is the reward of the factor but it is, cost of production to the producer. Productivity of the factor brings revenue to the producer. A producer will employ of factors upto the point where the marginal cost of the factor equals its marginal productivity. This will be the point of equilibrium because only this will be an ideal situation for the producer.

ii) Reward for each factor will be the same for every use the theory is based on the assumption of perfect mobility of factors. This process will continue until the productivity of a factor becomes equal in all its uses.

Similarly, the marginal productivity of all factor units is the same' in a particular firm or business. It is based on the assumption that all the factors are perfect'substitutes of each other. And the factors will be substituted for each other until their marginal productivity becomes equal. If a producer follows this law he will be having the maximum profits. Substitution of factors will take place till marginal products are equal.

The above mentioned 'substitution' is not only determined by 'marginal productivity' of factors, but also by the 'prices'. The equilibrium is reached only when marginal productivity as well as the prices of all the factors or of the same factors in different uses are equal.

The condition for achieving equilibrium can be states as:

$$\frac{\text{MRP of factor A}}{\text{Price of factor A}} = \frac{\text{MRP of factor B}}{\text{Price of factor B}}$$

iii) In the long run, under perfect competition each factor will get its remuneration equal to its MRP which also equals its ARP.

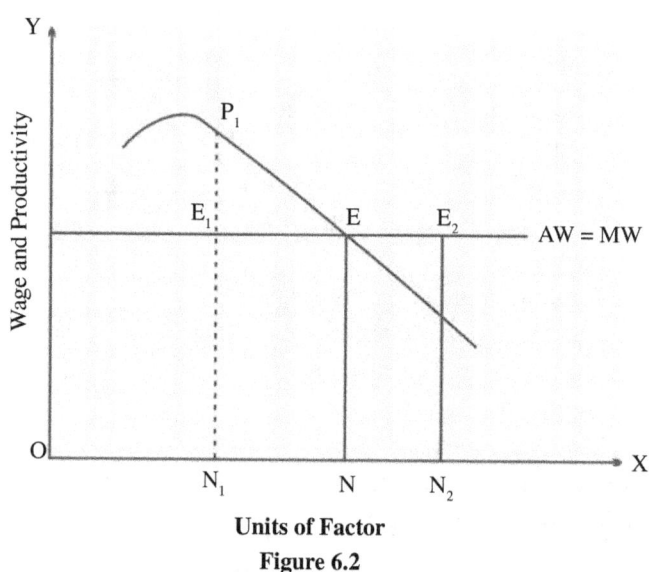

Units of Factor

Figure 6.2

Example : Labor as a factor : No single firm or producer can affect the price in perfect competition. So AR is always equal to MR (AR = MR). Similarly in factor market a single firm can not influence the wage rate which is determined by industry. At this wage rate, a firm can employ the required number of workers. Marginal productivity of labour is equal to average wages and marginal wages. It means supply curve of the factor (labour) is perfectly elastic i.e. horizontal straight line. To be in equilibrium, a producer compares the Marginal Wages- (MW) and Marginal Revenue Product (MRP). The producer will be in equilibrium where MRP = MW. It is explained with the help of below diagram.

In the above diagram at point E AW and MW are equal to MRP. The number of labourers employed is ON. Here the producer is in equilibrium.

Suppose the producer employs less workers i.e. ON_1. Here the MRP is $P_1 N_1$ but wage rate (AW) is N_1E_1 which is less than MRP P_1N_1 So the producer will employ more workers to increase production. If the producer employs ON_2 labourer, the MRP is N_2P_1. While wage rate is N_2 which is greater than the MRP. Here the producer suffers losses. So he will come back to N. It means he will employ ON labourers. In this way the producer is in equilibrium at point E and will get maximum profits by employing ON labourers. Here prices of factors are equal to their marginal productivity.

The Long Run Condition of Equilibrium

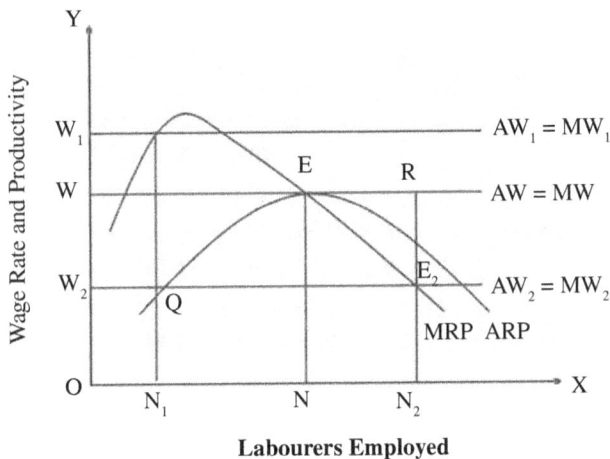

Figure 6.3

Here the MRP. ARP and wages are equal. In the above diagram - E is the equilibrium point where wage - rate AW = MW = MRP =ARP. Number of workers employed is ON. Here the firm is earning only 'Normal profits'. This is the long period output and price.

Suppose in short-run-wage rate is OW_1 at which the firm is suffering losses because wage rate is more than ARP by QE_1. Some firms will leave the market and the demand for workers will decrease. Wages will be reduced to OW. In the short run if wages are OW_2 equilibrium point will be E_2 where ON_2 workers will be employed. Here firms will be earning supernormal profits. For wage rate is less than ARP by E_2R. New Firms will be attracted and demand for workers will increase and push their price to OW. Hence in the long run, wages or factors reward is always equal to its ARP and MRP.

Criticism of the Margianl productivity Theory of Distribution :

1) The assumptions underlying the theory are unrealistc.
   (a) Perfect competition is not a reaslistic phenometion.
   (b) Factor units are never a line.
   (c) Factors ae perfectly mobile is not true. Also perfect divisibility of factors is not ture.
   (d) Assumption of full employment is also not true.
2) The theory explains wage determination and it has been exterded to determine the prices of other factors of production. However, every factor has its own choractenstics and accordingly their rewards are also fixed.
3) The theory ignores stort period.
4) The theory is one-sided. It only analyses the demand side of factor pricing and it ignores the supply side.
5) It is not possible to have a current measure of MRP.

6.2 RENT

Concept of Rent

In the ordinary sense rent means the payment paid to the owner for the use of house, machiness tractor, land etc. But in economics the term rent is used in different meaning. In economics the rent is that type of payment which is made to the owner of the land for the use of land. Modern economists say that rent is a surplus over opportunity cost which is calculated in case of any factor of production whose supply is inelastic.

Marshall defines Rent as *"the income derived from the ownership of land and* other *free gifts of nature."*

In the Ricardiansense *"rent is a payment by* a *tenant-farmer to the landlord for the use of the land."*

As per the Modern view, *"rent is a payment to any factor of production, over and above its transfer earning."*

Theories of Rent

i) The Ricardian Theory of Rent

David Ricardo a British economist, ideas on rent have a distinct place in economic theory. His views are known as the "Ricardian Theory of Rent". Ricardo said that rent is a 'surplus' which a accrues to the owners of land by reason of relative advantages of fertility or situation or both which a particular plot of land enjoys over 'les-productive' land-Ricarde defined rent like this.

"Rent is that portion of the produce of the earth which is paid to the landlord for the use of the original and indestructible powers of the soil." Hence rent is the price for use of land. It is paid to the owner of land. Land gets for its natural and non-perishable powers.

Assumptions of the Theory

Ricardian Theory of rent has its own assumptions. It assumes certain things about land, its supply and demand. The basic assumption underlying the theory are as follow:

i) *Fixed supply of land :* Ricardo assumed that we can't increase or decrease the existing quantity of land. It has been gifted and fixed by nature.

ii) *Original powers :* Second assumption underlying the theory is the original powers of land. It means that fertility or qualities of land are not the result of any type of human efforts. Rather they have been gifted by God.

iii) *Indestructible powers :* Ricardo's theory is also based on the idea that the powers or the qualities of earth are never destroyed. This means that a piece of land will have its fertility of the same type for ever. It will never diminish. Hence land is supposed to be a non-perishable factor of production.

iv) *Law of diminishing returns :* Ricardo, also, assumed the law of diminishing return or increasing costs operates in agriculture land.

v) *Cultivation in order of fertility :* The theory rests on the assumption that land is used in the order of its fertility and in fact order is diminishing. In other words, the most fertile land is used first and its next grade is used afterwards and so on.

vi) *Free gift :* Land is assumed to be a free gift of nature. God has provided it without taking any price. It has no cost of production.

vii) *Difference in fertility :* Ricardo also supposed that different lands have difference in their fertility some pieces of land are more fertile than the others.

viii) *Perfect competition :* The law is also based on the assumption of perfect competition.

ix) *Long run:* The theory is based on the assumption of long run.

x) *Marginal Land :* Marginal land is that land which is just covering its costs only i.e. income from it is equal to its costs.

xi) *Different situation :* Ricardo also supposed that various lands are located in different situations some are nearer to the market than the others.

Explanation of the Theory

According to Ricardo, there are various grades of land, differing from each other in respect of fertility and location. This differences in fertility lead to the factor yielding rent, i.e. superior and more fertile lands yield a surplus due to their differential advantages in production over inferior or less fertile land. Ricardo viewed rent as a differential surplus earned by more fertile plots of land in comparison with the less fertile plots of land. Therefore Ricardian theory of Rent is also called the differential theory of rent.

According to Ricardo Rent arises in both the techniques,

i. Extensive cultivation

ii. Intensive cultivation

i) Rent under extensive cultivation : Extensive cultivation is the type of farming under which production is increased by using more of land.

Ricardo took the case of an island where people go to settle. It is believed that no one is living before on this island. The land here is in excess in relation to the number of people who want to settle here. Because land is supposed to be a free gift of nature, so nothing has to be paid for its use. Again we suppose that there are four grades' land here i.e. A, B, C and D which have been written in the diminishing order of their fertility. This means that land 'A' is the most productive and 'D^1 the least productive. Now people who have come to settle will start farming to meet their demands of food etc. They will first all use type 'A' land, the most productive. 'A' grad land produces 35 tones of food grains per acre. When the demand for food grains increase, say due to fast increasing population the whole of land of grade 'A^1 will be utilized for farming. In order to meet this rising demand, people will start doing cultivation on B Type of land also. We assume that this land produces 30 tones of food grains. Land A will get a surplus i.e. Rent which is equal to their fertility difference {35 - 30 =5 tons). Land 'A' is called mtra-marginal land and the difference of produce between the marginal and inter-marginal land is called rent. Now if for some reason or the other, demand for foodgrain increase, people start cultivating the 'Type C land' also. Suppose it produces 15 tones per acre because it is less productive than grade A and B land. Now C is the marginal land while grades A & B are intra - marginal lands. A grade land will earn rent equal to the difference between its produce and that by of land C. If the demand for food increases the least productive land D will also be brought under cultivation say it gives 10 tone of production since it is the last to be cultivated, it will be called 'marginal Land' A , B and C types of land will be the 'Intra-marginal land'. These will be entitled to earn rents which is a surplus production over and above the production the marginal land D. The process discussed above can be shown through a table also.

Grade of Land	Production in tones (TR) (TR)	Surplus i.e. Rent in toes (TC)
A	35	35 – 10 = 25
B	30	30 – 10 = 20
C	15	15 – 10 = 05
D	10	10 – 10 = 0

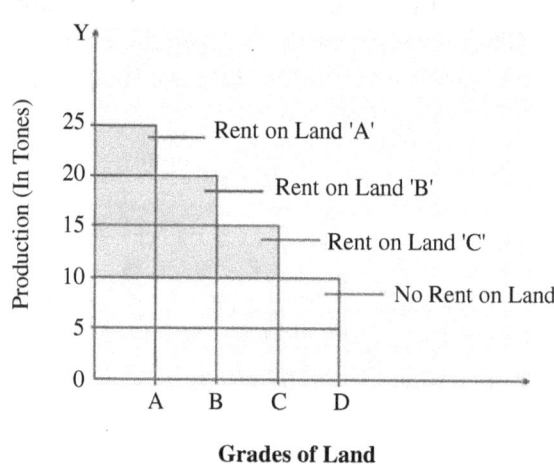

Grades of Land

Figure 6.4

The table given above shows that grades A, B and C of land earn rents of 25, 20 and 5 tons of produce respectively. The D type of land earns no rent. It is called marginal land. The rent earned by A, B and C type of land are the surpluses which they produce in relation to D grade land which is the last to be used.

It can be illustrated through above figure.

In this diagram the amount of rent earned A, B and C grades of lands are shown by the differently shaded areas. D grade land just covers its costs or is the last to be used. So it is 'No-

Rent Land'. Hence rent under extensive cultivation is a surplus between the production of the marginal and the intra-marginal lands.

ii) Rent under intensive cultivation : Under intensive cultivation on the same piece of land, more units of labour and capital are employed to increase production wote that Ricardo used the assumption of the operation of the 'diminishing returns' on agriculture. It means that production increase at a diminishing rate when more and more units of labour and capital are employed on the given piece of land. The law leads us to the conclusion that rent also arises even when all plots of land are alike in fertility and situation. Ricardo's argument is simple to follow.

When more and more units of labour and capital are put to work on the same piece of land, production increases at diminishing rate. Hence marginal product will go on diminishing, marginal product refers to the addition made to total production by using one more unit of labour and capital, other factor units remaining constant. Example that four such units i.e. 1st, 2nd, 3rd and 4th are put to work and they prodtice 25, 20, 15 and 10 tones of marginal product respectively. To make it clear when the 1st unit of labour and capital is used it makes an addition of 25 tons to total production. By using 2nd, 3rd and 4th units, additions to total production of 20, 15, and 10 tons are made respectively. Because the 4th unit of labour and capital is the last to be used it is called the marginal units of labour and capital. It is also called 'No rent unit'. The other three units i.e: 1st, 2nd 3rd are producing more than the last. Hence they earn rent and are called the Intra- marginal units. Their rent is equal to the difference between their production and that of the last unit i.e. the 4th. These facts can also put in the form of a table given below.

Units of Labour and Capital	Production in tones (TR)	Surplus of Rent in tones (TC)
1st	25	25-10 = 15
2nd	20	20-10 = 10
3rd	15	15-10 = 05
4th	10	10-10 = 00

The table given above shows that the 1st, 2nd and 3rd units of labour and capital earn rent, not due to the difference of the fertility of land, but due to diminishing returns, to variable factors on the same piece of land. This concept is explained with the help of following diagram :

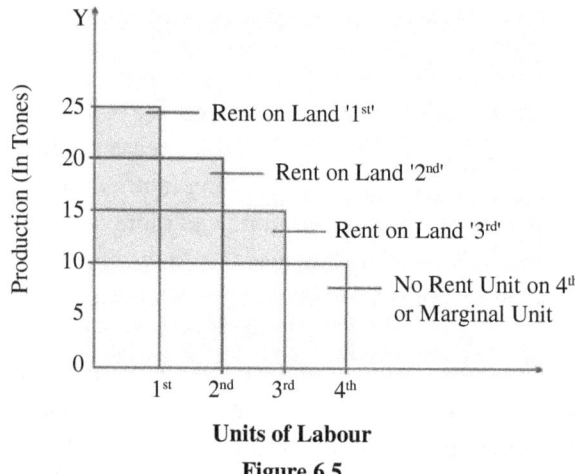

Figure 6.5

The diagram shows that even on the land of given fertility and situation, rent can arise by intensive cultivation when more and more units of labour and capital are used on them. This is due to, law of diminishing returns. That is why, in the diagram, units 1st, 2nd and 3rd earn rent in the shape of 'surplus' which are difference between their production and production of the last used unit. The 1st, 2nd and 3rd units earn (25 - 10 = 15)(, (20 - 10 = 10), (15 10 = 05) tons of produce as rent respectively.

Hence rent was a surplus which the intra-marginal lands and units of labour and capital earn over and above the production of marginal units of labout and capital or marginal lands.

Criticism of Ricardian Theory of Rent

i) Ricardo's'view of the concept of rent as a payment made for the use of original and indestructible powers of soil is incorrect. Moreover, in the modern era, one cannot claim anything to be indestructible.

ii) Ricardo believed that rent is differential surplus. But he ignored the other type of rent which arises not only due to the fertility and situational difference but also due to the scarcity of land. But actually, rent arises because the demand for land is much more than its supply.

iii) Ricardo assumed the prevalence of perfect competition. But it never exists in the real world. Since there is imperfect competition for land the rent charged by the landowners is more than the economic rent.

iv) Ricardo meant by the rent the income of the landowner from the use of original and indestructible powers of land marginal land, was formed as 'No Rent Land[1]. In other words, marginal land is without its original and indestructible powers.

v) *Rent element in all factors :* Ricardo entitled only land to earn rent because he believed that supply is perfectly inelastic. But modern economies criticized this narrow concept of rent According to them rent is not the income of land only.

vi) Ricardian theory only states the idea that since more fertile lands produce more than the least fertile pieces they earn a surplus known as Rent. But it does not determine how and where rent is fixed.

vii) Another criticism against the theory is that the law of diminishing return does not always operate. In the present world, with the help of improved technology, production increases rather at increasing rate as more and more units of the factors are employed.

ii) Modern Theory of Rent

Modern theory of rent is an improvement or modification over the Ricardian theory of rent.

In the Ricardian theory rent was linked only with land i.e. only land could earn rent. Its reason as given by Ricardo is that the supply of land is perfectly inelastic. We can't change it. Secondly, various lands differ in fertility, more fertile lands, of course, produce more than the marginal land. So these have an advantage over the less productive lands. The surpluses which the farmer produce is called rent by Ricardo.

But modern economists have made it clear that the two qualities of land namely its inelastic supply and differences in Fertility, are also .found among the other factors of production. In the short run the supply of labour, capital and entrepreneur is also limited and is less in relation to their demand. Their supply is difficult to alter in the short period. Similarly, the second quality of land is also favoured among the factors other than land. Just as lands differ in fertility, different factors of production have different efficiencies and productivity. The supply of these more productive factors is less elastic or even inelastic. Hence, as per modern theory is not only land which can earn rent but other factors of production i.e. labour, capital organization and entrepreneur are also entitled to earn rent. Land is scarce. So it earns scarcity rent. Lands differ in Fertility so they earn differential rents.

Ricardian theory explains only that the more fertile lands produce more than the cost of cultivation and hence they get a surplus called 'Rent'. But how is rent determined. This question was not answered by Ricardian theory. Modern economists have developed a demand and supply theory 'for the purpose. Hence modern economists are of the opinion that like the prices of products and other factors, rent is also determined by the forces of demand and supply. The theory is also known as 'scarcity theory of Rent'. The theory explains that rent does not arise due to fertility differences of land alone but due to more demand in relation to the supply of all factors. Hence the forces of demand and supply together determine rent. Hence we will now study the nature of forces of demand and supply of land.

i) **Demand side:** The demand for land is indirect or derived. In fact, land is demanded for it produces something. The higher the demand for the goods produced on land, the demand for land will also go up and therefore the price of the service of land (Rent) will be higher.

Marginal productivity of land determines the demand for it. As we go on investing more and more on the same land, its marginal productivity goes on declining. So land will be demanded only up to that point where marginal productivity of land equals its cost of cultivation. We can also say that more land will be demanded at lower rent. Hence the demand curve for land slopes downward from left to right.

ii) Supply side : The supply of land can't be altered for the society as whole. Increased rent can't increase its supply. Nor the fall in its price can decrease its supply. Land is given to mankind by nature. Land has alternative uses i.e. it can be used in several ways so, for a particular industry or firm or individual the supply of land can be changed, i.e. it is elastic. Any individual can get more land by bidding up its price. Hence the supply curve of land for an individual firm or industry is having an 'upward slope'.

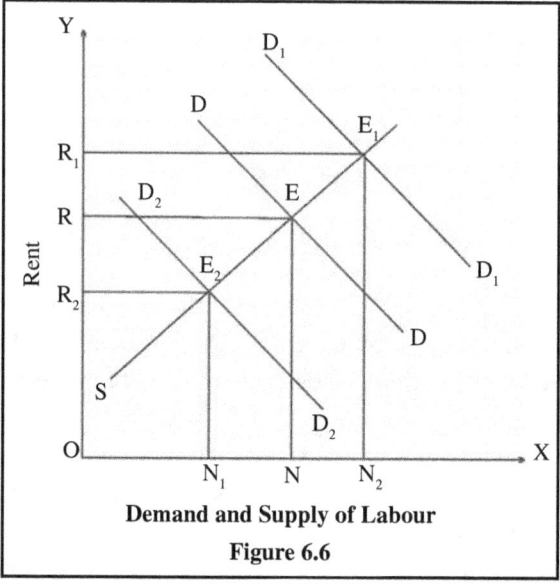

Demand and Supply of Labour

Figure 6.6

Rent is determined at the point where demand for and supply of land intersect each other. This is shown through a diagram given above.

In Figure DD' and SS' as the demand and supply curves of land respectively. The equilibrium point for the industry is E where demand and supply of land are equal and the curves cut each other. Here land demanded and supplied is ON and the price of the use of land (i.e. Rent) is fixed at OR. Now suppose, for some reason or the other, the demand for land increase its price for use also goes upward to OR, because the higher demand curve DjD, cuts the supply curve at point E, on the other hand a fall in demand as shown by D_2D_2 leads to fall in rent at the level OR_2.

iii) Rent as a surplus : Ricardo considered rent as a surplus earned by the intra-marginal lands which is over and above the production of the marginal lands. Modern economists agree to the idea of the surplus being rent. But they differ on the point that rent is earned only by land. Modern economists are of the opinion that other factors of production than land can also earn rent. The factor of in-elasticity of supply is also found among other factors of production in the short-run. For *example,* the supply of labour, capital and entrepreneurs cannot be changed in the short run so they also earn over and above their 'normal income'. This surplus is in the nature of rent.

iv) Rent and transfer earnings : Modern Economists have defined rent 'as a surplus' earned by the factors which is over and above their. Transfer Earning'. Transfer earning is means the amount of income which a particular factor could earn in its next best or alternative use. Transfer earning is also called the minimum price of a factor. In other words, transfer earning refers to the price which a factor unit must get in its present use in order to stay in its present employment otherwise he will shift in his job. Hence transfer earning can be defined as the price which is necessary to keep a factor unit in its present use. The income which a factor actually gets from its present work or job is called its 'Actual Earning'. The surplus which a factor earns over its transfer earning is known as Economics rent. Hence we can say that if actual earning of a factor exceeds its transfer earning the surplus earning is rent.

Therefore Rent = Actual Earning – Transfer Earning

v) Supply elasticity of factors and rent : According to the modern theory of rent as a surplus over transfer earning, depends on the elasticity of supply of the Factors. The three types of elasticity and the rents earned by them can be explained as follows.

i) *Supply perfectly inelastic (Es = zero) :* The main cause for the emergence of economic rent is the scarcity of the factor of production. It means that the transfer earning of a factor-unit is determined by the elasticity of supply. If the elasticity of supply is zero, that is supply of a factor of production is perfectly inelastic, the transfer earning will be zero. Because the factor of production cannot be transferred to any other use. The same amount of factor-units are supply irrespective of its price, in this case theminimum supply price is zero. This may be explained with the help of figure.

In the diagram below *(Figure 6.7) SS is* the perfectly inelastic supply curve and demand curve DD. Equilibrium factor price = OP and OR is the number of factor units demanded and supplied, The total earning are shown by a □OPQR. Transfer earnings being zero, earning indicate economic rent. So in this entire earnings are in the form of rent shown by a □OPQR.

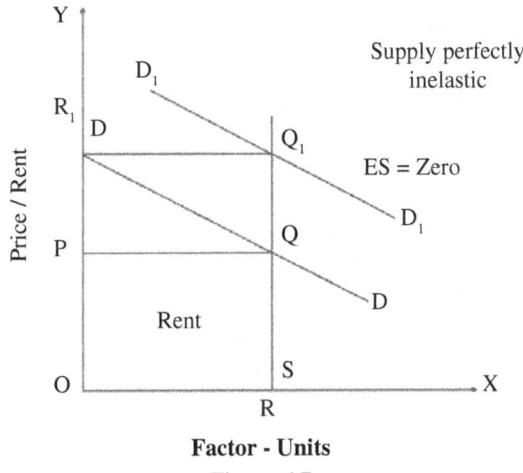

Factor - Units
Figure 6.7

ii) *Perfectly Elastic Supply (ES = ∞):* When the elasticity of supply is equal to infinity, which means supply is perfectly elastic, the factor of production earn no rent. Its entire earnings are transfer earning as shown in Figure.

In the Figure, we have drawn the supply curve SS parallel to Ox-axis to indicate perfectly elastic supply, which any amount of factor-units means can be had but at the same wage rate. Supply being perfectly elastic, entire earning become transfer earning of the factor of production. DD demand curve cuts SS supply curve at point E. Price or rent is fixed at OP. Actual earning are shown by □OPEM. Transfer earnings are equal to actual earning shown by □OPEM. If demand curye shift upward to D₁D₁ Actual earning also increase to □OPE₁M₁. Hence

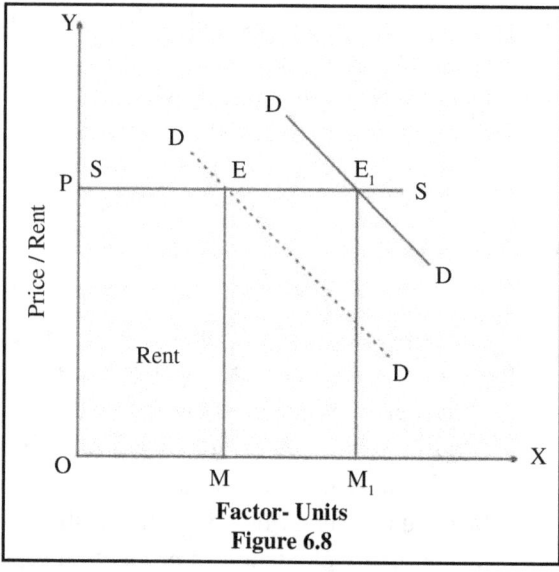

Factor- Units

Figure 6.8

when a factor is perfectly elastic in supply. It can't earn rent.

iii) *Supply less than perfectly elastic:* If the supply of a factor is relatively inelastic the income of a factor of production will contain transfer earning and also an element of rent. This can be'illustrated as follows.

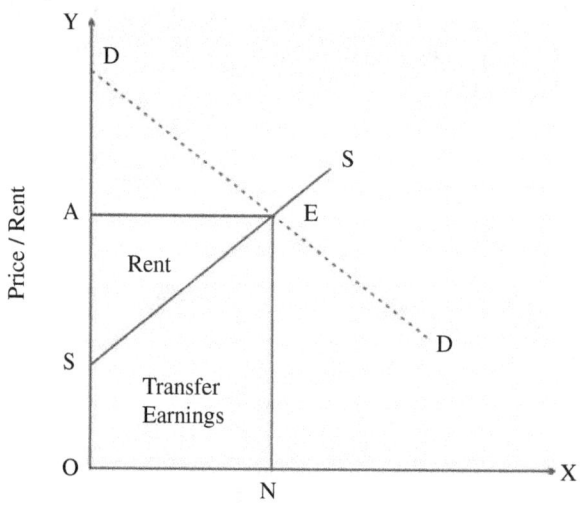

Factor - Units

Figure : 6.9

In *figure* SS is the supply curve, which has an upward slop i.e. supply rises at a higher price. DD demand curve intersect the supply curve at point E and rent is determined at OA and supply of factor-units is ON. In short;

Total Earnings = OAEN

Total Transfer Earnings = OSEN

Economic Rent = AES.

Summary chart conclusion of the modern Theory of Rent

Particulars of Supply	Conclusion
i. When supply is perfectly inelastic.	Entire-earning-Rent.
ii. When supply is perfectly elastic.	Entire earnings -Transfer Earnings.
iii. Supply less than perfectly elastic.	Earnings contain both economic rent and Transfer Earnings.

6.3 WAGES

Labour is a human factor and the payment made to the labour for his mental and physical work is called wages. In economics mental or physical labour for which payment made is called labour.

The term 'wage' means payments made to the labourers for their services, because it helps in production.

Concept of Money Wages or Nominal Wages and Real Wages

Money wages is also called nominal wages. Money wage means the payment made to workers in terms of money. *For example,* a labour is paid Rs. 100 per day then it is called money wages. Money wages is calculated in terms of money paid either for mental labour or physical labour to worker.

Real wages : When the money wages are expressed in term of goods and service and the facilities provided by an employer to the workers. In other words, real wages means money wages plus other facilities given to the worker like housing facility, free electricity facilities and conveyance given by the employer; to the workers.

Thus, real wages are calculated on the basis of the following formula.

Real wages = Money Wage in terms of goods and services other facilities provided by the employer.

Factors Determining Real Wage

Factors that determine real wage are as follows:

i. *Price level :* Real wage and price level are inversely related. When the prices are high, the purchasing capacity of money goes down and the real wage falls.

ii. *Working conditions :* Comfortable work place, flexible working hours, friendly colleagues and understanding superiors will give job satisfaction and increase real wage.

iii. *Job risks :* A risky job will not give high real wage even if the money wage is high.

iv. *Extra earnings :* In some jobs extra earnings are possible. *For example,* a teacher can earn more through tuitions. Such jobs may have low money wage but will carry high real wage.

v. *Fringe benefits :* Some jobs carry benefits like housing, transportation, medical, educational-allowances, etc. These per quisites will increase real wage. Retirement benefits like pension will also increase real wage.

vi. *Promotion chances :* A job in which it is possible to get quick promotions and higher status will have more real wage.

vii. *Cost of training and trade expenses :* Education for professions like that of a doctor, CA takes a long period. The training before taking up regular job is also long. Hence the real wage of such profession is comparatively low.

viii. *Other factors :* Some jobs offer a lot of honour and social prestige.
In some there are chances for foreign travel. Such jobs have high real wage.

Backword Sloping Supply Curve of Labour

The supply of labour means the number of workers who are ready to work on prevailing wage rate. Mandays and hours of work are the variables on which the supply of labour depends.

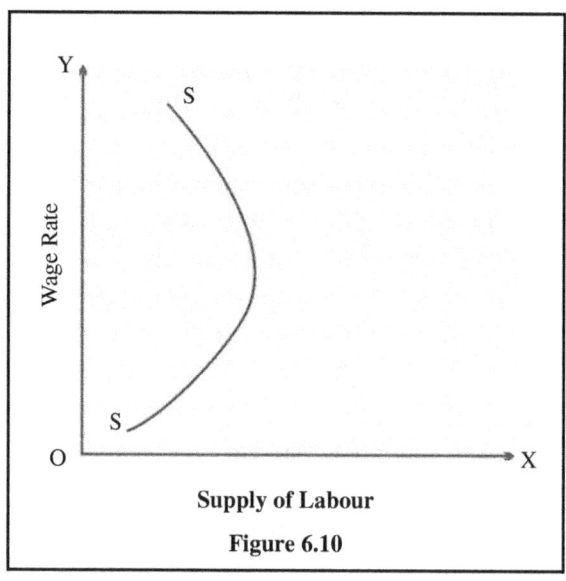

Supply of Labour

Figure 6.10

The supply of labour is affected by social, economic and political factors in an economy. The size of population, age group and sex-ratio determine the supply of labour. The supply of labour is also affected by the hours of work and leisure preference of workers on a given wage rate during a given period. In the beginning there may be a direct relation between wage rate and the supply of labour. Higher is the wage rate higher will be the supply and low is the wage rate low will be the supply of labour. But after a point there will be backward bending of supply of labour because when workers have satisfied their wants not only necessaries but also comforts then they will prefer to have more of leisure and less of work. The relation between wage rate and supply of labour can be studied with the help of the following diagram.

There is direct relationship between the wage rate and the supply of labour. After a point there is backward bending of supply curve because workers prefer leisure and work less.

Collective Bargaining

The trade union makes an agreement with the employer determining wage and other conditions. This is done through discussion and negotiations. This is known as collective

Bargaining. Since the trade union represents all the workers, the benefits secured by the collective bargaining reach all the workers.

Wage Determination and Collective Bargaining

The trade union plays an important role in determining, the wages and other benefits to the labourers. It follows the given methods for this purpose.

i) *By restricting the supply of labour :* The union restricts labour supply by fixing lesser number of working hours. It also works to restrict immigration of workers from other states and countries. It also forces the industry to stop new recruitment.

So as seen in diagram, when the supply curve of labor reduces thenthe equilibrium between demand and supply of labour rises to E_1 and the wages increase to OW_1.

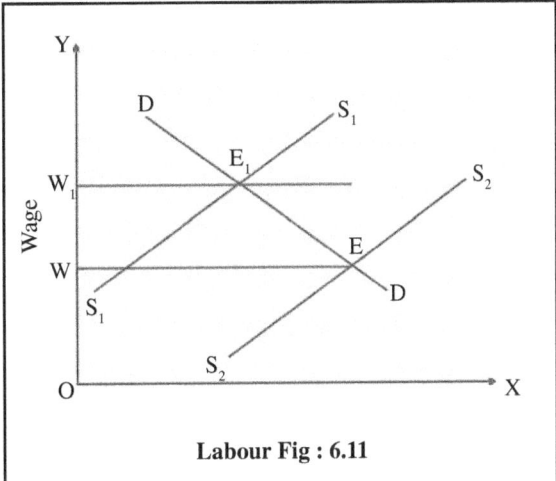

Labour Fig : 6.11

ii) *By increasing the demand for labour in the industry :* It is not very easy to increase the demand for labour off hand. So the union takes the given two steps.

a. Labourers are given skill through education and technical training. This increase their marginal productivity. This in turn increase their demand,

b. Demand for product is increased through heavy advertising and by giving liberal concessions. When the demand rises the wages also increase.

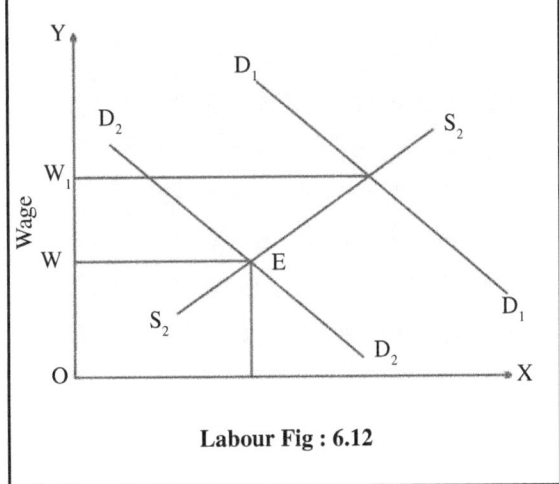

Labour Fig : 6.12

iii) *By showing the strength of the union wages can be increased :* Under perfect competitive conditions, the wage curve or the supply curve of labour is a horizontal straight line ON workers are employed

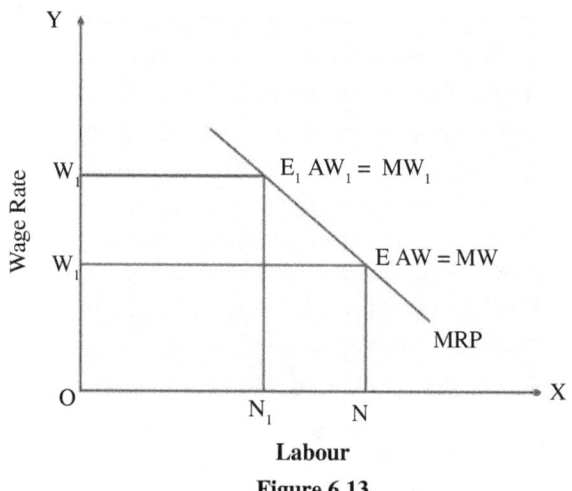

Figure 6.13

E shows the point when the MRP line cuts the supply curve and AW = MW. So wages are OW.

The union can bargain for a higher wage rate at the equilibrium E_1, at which $AW_1 = MW_1$. So wages rise to OW_1. But at this wage the labour supply is reduced to ON_1.

Thus the labour is very much dependent on the bargaining strength of the trade unions for its welfare.

6.4 INTEREST

Interest is regarded as the reward or payment for the use of capital to the owner of capital. Modern production is based on division of labour and specialization in which huge amount of capital is required payment made for the use of capital is called interest.

Definitions of Interest

Different economists have defined interest some of these definitions are given below:

  i) **Prof. J.S. Mill has defined,** *"Interest is the remuneration for mere abstinence."*

 ii) **Prof. Meyers,** *"Interest is the price paid for the use of loanable funds."*

iii) **Prof. Alfred Marshall has defined.** *"Interest its the price of use of capital in any market."*

Thus, the above definition reveal that interest is the payment for the use of capital of money made by the borrower.

Gross Interest and Net Interest

Economists have differentiated the meaning of gross & net interest. The total amount which a creditor gets from the debtor is called the gross interest. The components of the gross interest is as follows:

  i) *Pure or net interest :* It is the payment made for the use of capital only. This is the interest in true economic sense.

ii) *Reward for Risk :* When lender lends money he takes risks. These risks are divided into two parts.

    a) Trade risks depends upon the nature of the business in which the capital is used.

    b) Personal risks are due to the dishonest or unreliable character of the borrower himself. The lender therefore, expects a reward in proportion to the degree of risks.

iii) *Reward for management :* Every lender has to incur some expenditure an management of loan. He has to maintain staff and buy accounts books so lender needs same reward for this work.

iv) *Reward for Inconvenience :* When a lender lends money he loses his command over it for a specific period it can not be used in more profitable ways. The compensation for such Inconvenience is added to the interest charged.

Gross Interest = Net Interest + Insurance

Against Risk + Wages for Management + Reward for Inconvenience

i) Theories of Interest

This is also called the Neo-Classical theory of interest. According to this theory, *"the rate of interest is detemine by the demand for and supply of loanable funds"* Loanable funds are the sums of money supplied in the market.

Let us now analyse the supply of and the demand for the loanable funds in the credit market.

Supply of Loanable Funds

The four major sources of supply of loanable funds the are:

i) *Saving (S) :* The main source of supply of loanable funds is saving. Saving is the part of income which is not spent on consumption. Saving depend mainly upon two things:

    a. Size of income

    b. Rate of interest

    In this theory it is assumed that size of income remains the same. So only rate of interest affects savings. Higher rate of interest gives incentive to people to save more. On the contrary, at a lower interest rate, people save less. In this way, supply is done not only by individuals but also by firm. Like individual, firms also save more at a higher rate of interest and vice versa.

    Therefore, supply curve of loanable funds from savings slopes upward from left to right. This is shown by the curve S in Figure.

ii) *Dishoarding (DH):* Hoarded money is the money kept in cash by the people; when rate of interest rises, people dishoard their cash money. They supply it for loanable funds. When interest rate is high, people want to earn more interest. So higher rate of interest induces people to dishoard their money. On the contrary, a fall in the rate of interest or a low interest rate will lead people to hoard more money. This is a direct relationship between the rate of interest and dishoarding. That is why the dishoarding curve, shown by DH curve in figure, slopes upward from left to right.

iii) *Bank Money (BM) :* The third important source of supply of loanable funds is bank money. By accepting deposits, giving loans and through the purchase and sale of securities, commercial banks create credit. In this way, they supply loanable funds. Generally, banks lend more at high rate of interest and less at low rate of interest. Therefore, the supply curve of bank money (BM) is shown in the diagram to be sloping upward to the right. It is directly linked with the rate of interest.

iv) *Disinvestment (DI):* Disinvestment is an important source of supply of loanable funds. There are some firms incurring losses. In other words, in these firms marginal productivity of capital is lower than the market rate of interest. In such a situation. These firms withdraw their capital from business and lend it. In this way, people, in order to earn the rate of interest, withdraw their previously-done investment. At higher rate of interest, disinvestment is also inversely related to the rate of investment. Supply curve DI as shown in the figure slopes upward to the right.

We can get the total supply curve of loanable funds by a lateral summation of the curves of saving (S), dishoarding (DH), bank money (BM) and disinvestment (DI). The aggregate supply curve of loanable funds SL also slopes upward to the right. It shows the direct relationship between the rate of interest and supply of loanable funds.

Demand for Loanable Funds

The demand for loanable funds arises mainly from three sources.

i) *Investment Demand (I) :* The main source of demand for loanable funds is the demand for investment. Investment means expenditure of funds on building new and fresh capital goods. Rate of interest is the cost of borrowing funds for investment. A person will go an borrowing or demanding money for investment up to the point where cost of borrowing it. We know that marginal productivity of investment diminishes with every increase in investment. So a businessman is prepared to demand more loanable funds for investment only at lower rate of interest. In other words, the demand for funds for investment rises with a fall in the rate of interest. So there is an inverse relationship between the rate of interest and demand for funds for investment. That is why the demand curve for investment (I) as show in figure A slopes downward from left to right.

ii) *Consumption Demand (C) :* People also demand loanable funds for consumption purposes, sometimes people want to purchase goods which are beyond the reach of their own incomes. So to get them, they demand loanable funds.

For example, a person whose monthly income is Rs. 10,000 per month wants to buy a refrigerator. In order to buy it he will demand loanable funds. The demand for lonable fund for consumption purposes is also related with the rate of interest. There is an inverse relationship between consumption demand and rate of interest the demand curve for loanable funds, for consumption (C) as shown in Figure A slopes downward from left to right.

iii) *Demand for Hoarding (H) :* Third source of demand for loanable funds is for hoarding purposes. Hoarding means keep money in idle cash. It is a natural interest in human beings that they want to keep some money with them in ready cash its simple reason is that ready or cash money has an advantage over other forms of keeping money in securities, bonds, shares and banks etc. Cash money can be utilized at any time according to our own desire. That is why people demand money for hoarding it. It is also interest elastic. At a higher rate of interest people want to hoard less. At higher interest rate they will lend more money i.e. they will-supply loanable funds to get the benefits of interest on the contrary at lower rate of interest, people will desire to keep more money with them in cash rather than giving it in loans. So demand of loanable funds for hoarding is also inversely related to the rate of interest. Therefore demand curve for hoarding which is shown in the figure as H curve also slopes downward from left to right.

In order to get the total demand or aggregate demand for loanabled funds, we have to add the three demand curves horizontally i.e. Investment curve (I), consumption curve (C) and Hoarding curve (H). In this way we get an aggregate demand curve for loanable funds. It is shown by DL in the right hand side of the same diagram. It slopes downward from left to right.

Loanable funds theory explains that the equilibrium rate of interest is determined by the id interaction of the forces of demand for and supply of loanable funds. Where the demand and supply of loanable funds are equal to each other, rate of interest is determined. This is shown through the diagram of *figure 6.14.*

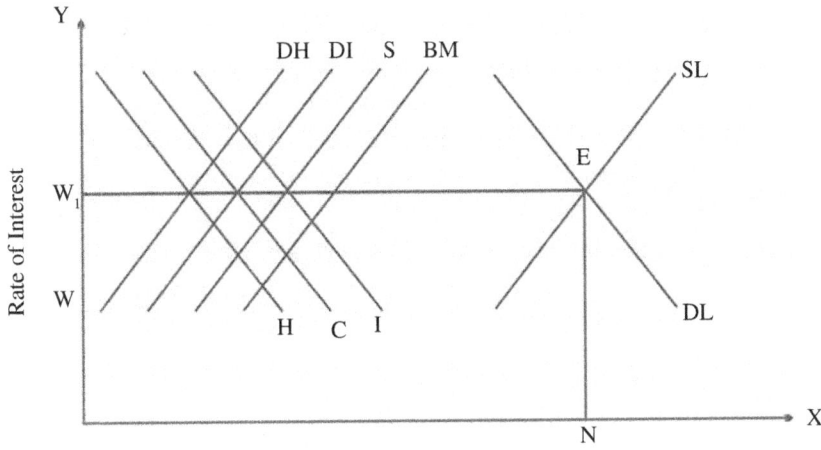

Figure 6.14 : Determination of the rate of interest through Loanable Funds Theory

In *Figure 6.14* H, C and I are the demand curves for loanable funds for hoarding, consumption and investment respectively. DH, DI, S and BM are the supply curves from dishoarding, disinvestment, Saving and bank money. By the horizontal summation of H, C and I. We get an aggregate demand curve for loanable funds as shown by DL curve in the figure. SL is the supply curve of loanable funds. It has also resulted from the summation of DH. DI, S and BM curves respectively. The aggregative demand curve and supply curves of loanable funds cut each other at point E. This, the equilibrium rate of interest or gets determined.

ii) Keynes Liquidity Preference Theory of Interest

Lord Keynes has developed a new theory of interest known as Liquidity preference theory of interest. It is called the Liquidity preference theory of interest because Keynes Explains Interest as "that price for parting with Liquidity" According to him, interest is purely a monetary phenomenon. It is a payment for the use of money or the price for parting; with liquidity. He defines interest as "the premium which has to be offered to induce people to hold their wealth in same from other than hoarded money" In other words, interest is the opportunity cost of holding cash.

According to this theory the rate of interest is determined by the demand for and the supply of money.

Demand for Money (Liquidity Preference)

People have a very strong desire to hold money as it is the most liquid asset available to them. Money can be put to any use immediately and therefore people demand money. The desire of people to hold money is called the "Liquidity preference". Keynes maintains that people desire to hold money or demand for three motives or three purposes.

They are:
i) Transactions Motive
ii) Precautionary Motive
iii) Speculative Motive

i) Transactions Motive : People need a certain amount of money for meeting their day to day transactions. The demand for money for current transactions is called the transactions demand for motive. Since income is received periodically liquid balance are necessary to bridge the gap between receipt of income and expenditure. A person who gets his salary once in a months must keep enough cash in his hands to meet payments of everyday transactions. For *example,* a person travelling by local bus to attend his job everyday will have to set side a certain amount of cash for meeting his everyday bus fare. Similarly those who get their wages once in a week may hold some cash for meeting current transactions such as purchasing of fresh vegetables, buying of milk or fish, etc., same in the case even with business houses. There may be a gap between business expenses and sales receipts. Firms under such conditions are required to keep liquid money for financing day to day transactions.

The amount of money required for this purpose depends upon the level of income, intervals at which incomes are received, spending habits, general level of business activity and the methods of payment existent in locality.

We come to the conclusion that demand for money for transaction motive mainly depend on the size of income. More money will be demanded at higher levels of income and vice-versa. So transaction demand for money or liquidity is income elastic we can express this conclusion in the form of an equation also.

$$M, = f(y)$$

where　　M_l　　= Demand for Liquidity for transaction motive,

　　　　　$f(y)$　= refers to be function of income

ii) Precautionary Motive : People may desire to hold money to meet certain unforeseen and sudden expenditures. Everyone likes to take precaution against certain contingent liabilities and unforeseen expenses. Such a demand for money is called the precaution demand for money. In other words, the precautionary motive relates, to the desire to have available for future requirement and unforeseen contingencies a certain proportion - of total resources in the form of cash. For instance, a marriage ceremony in the neighbours house requires gift to be purchased which, is an item of sudden expenditure. Similarly emergencies like. Sickness and accidents. To meet such sudden expenditure people have a desire to hold some money in the form of cash or readily withdrawable deposits in banks. Keynes call this as the precautionary motive for money. Like individuals business concerns also face emergencies and have contingent and unforeseen liabilities. Therefore, they also keep a portion of their income in the form of reserve to meet sudden expenditures.

We can say that demand for liquidity for precautionary motive depends upon the size of income, nature of persons, and farsightedness etc. It is also income-elastic like the demand for money transaction motive. Higher is the level of income, the greater will be the demand for money for precautionary motive. The relation can also be expressed in an equation as given below.

$$M_2 = f(y)$$

Here M_2 refers to demand for money for precautionary motive, F(Y) refers to the function of income.

Since both the transaction and precautionary motives for holding cash depend upon income Keynes put them together because both these motives are income-elastic they can be expressed through a joint equation given below.

$$M_1 + M_2 - L_1 f(y)$$

where

M_1 = Demand for money for transaction motive

M_2 = Demand for money for precautionary motive.

By adding M_1 and M_2 we get L_1 which refers to the demand for money on account of transaction and precautionary motives. f(y) means the function of income.

iii) Speculative Motive : The speculative demand for money relates to he desire of people to hold resources in liquid form with a view to take the advantage of market movements. People desire to hold cash in anticipation of earning profits in future. According to Keynes, it is this motive which primarily involves the propensity to hoard. The

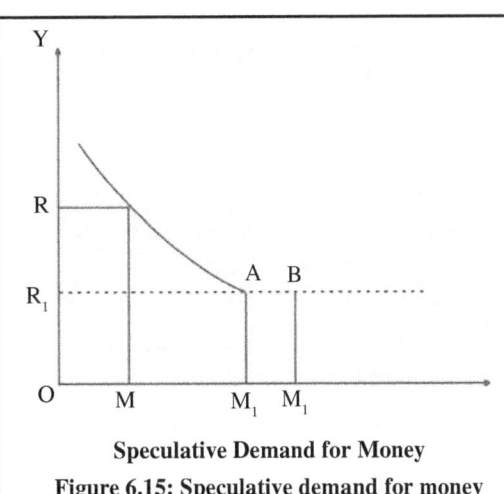

Speculative Demand for Money

Figure 6.15: Speculative demand for money

object is to secure better profits by anticipating changes in future. This tendency is the common feature of the stock exchange. A stock exchange is a market where sale and purchase of shares, bonds and securities take place. Sometimes there will be excessive purchase of securities if is called the 'Bullish sentiment' and the tendency for aggressive sale of securities is known as the 'Bearish sentiment'.

Such a speculative demand for money is highly sensitive to the changes in rate of interest. The speculative demand, Keynes emphasized this motive this speculative money demand function is shows as

$$L_2 = f(r)$$

Where, L_2 is the speculative demand for money

f(r) refers to the function of rate of interest.

There is inverse relationship between the-rate of interest and demand for liquidity for satisfying the speculative motive. The speculative demand for money can be illustrated as follows.

In the above diagram (Figure 6.15) LPC indicates the (Liquidity Preference for Speculation) speculative demand for money. At interest rate OR, the speculative demand for money is OM. When rate of interest falls from OR to OR_1 the speculative demand for money increase from OM to OM_1. Rate of interest cannot fall below this minimum limit. This minimum level of the rate of interest is shown by the AB portion of the liquidity preference curve. Where portion AB of the LPC curve is parallel to X-axis. It shows that when the rate of interest is R_1 liquidity preference is OM. Even if the money supply increases from OM_1 to OM_2, rate of interest will not fall below OR_1 So OR_1 is the minimum limit of the rate of interest. AB portion of the liquidity preference curve showing the lowest limit of the interest rate is popularly called liquidity trap. The liquidity trap tells us that the money of interest can never tall to either zero or a negative level.

Such a speculative demand for money is highly sensitive to the changes in rate of interest. The speculative demand, therefore, is dependent on the rate of interest. The rate of interest and bond prices are inversely related. Let us suppose that an individual intends to purchase a bond of Rs. 5000. Further assume that the rate of interest is 4 percent. Now on this bond he earns the income of Rs. 200 p.a. when the rate of interest goes up to 5 percent, to earn the same income of Rs. 200 investment of Rs. 4000 is sufficient It means bond price decrease with an increases in the rate of interest and vice versa. This shows that when the rate of interest is higher, people will have a desire to hold less money for speculative purposes. People invest money in bonds with the fall in interest rates. When the rate of interest decreases, the bond holders sell their bonds and hold liquid cash. It means that lower the rate of interest, greater will be the liquidity preference. Thus speculators buy bonds when their prices are lower and sell them when they get a higher price.

Hence liquidity preference for speculative motive varies inversely with the rate of interest.

Supply of Money

Supply of money is quite different from the demand for money. Supply of money is not interest- elastic in the short run. No private individual can change it. Supply of money is controlled by the central bank of a country or its Government. Money supply depends upon the currency issued by the Government and the policy followed by the central bank of the country regarding credit creation. In the short run i.e. at a particular period of time supply of money remains constant that is why, the supply curve of money is perfectly inelastic which means its being parallel to OY-axis as is shown in Figure 6.16.

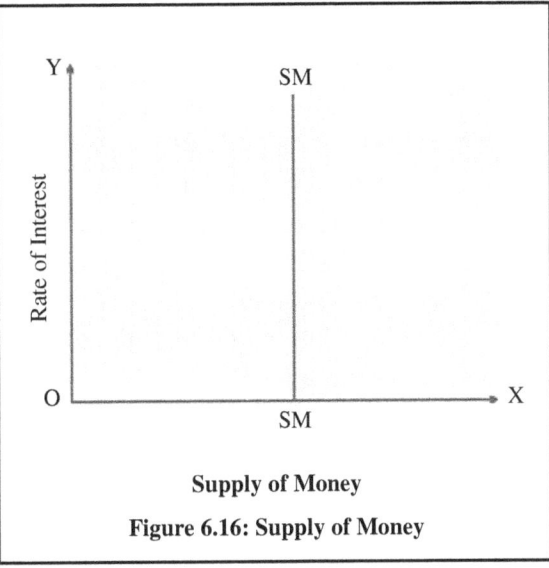

Supply of Money

Figure 6.16: Supply of Money

The diagram shows supply of money on X - axis and the rate of interest on Y-axis. SM-SM, is the supply curve of money. It is parallel to the Y - axis. It shows that supply of money remains constant, in the short-run period and changes in rate of interest does not affect supply of money.

Determination of the Rate of Interest

Keynes pointed out that rate of interest is determined at a point where demand for money is equal to the supply of money. In other words, equilibrium between the forces of demand for money and supply of money determine the rate of interest.

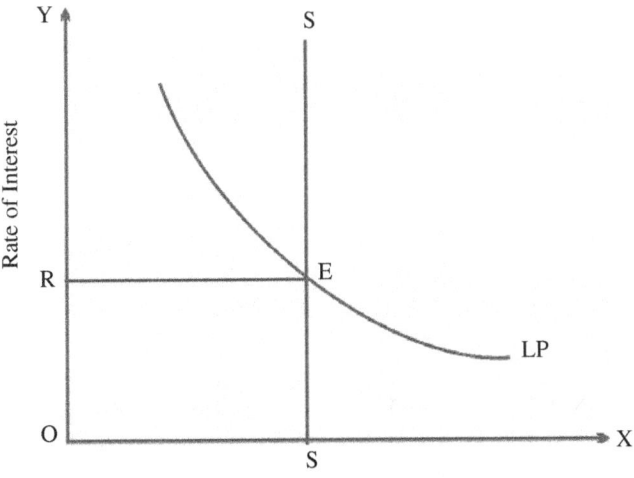

Demand for and Supply of Money

Figure 6.17: Determination of the Rate of Interest

So we can say that

The Equilibrium rate of interest is found when

$$M = Sm.$$

where   M = Total demand for money

Sm = Supply of money

The determination of rate interest can be show through a diagram such as in Figure 6.17.

In the above (Figure 6.17) SS indicates the inelastic supply curve of money and the curve LP indicates the liquidity preference for speculative motive. They intersect at E and the equilibrium rate of interest OR is determined. At this rate of interest of demand for money equals supply of money (OS).

Changes in demand for money

With supply remaining constant, any change in the liquicity preference tends to alter the rate of interest. When the liquidity preference curve shift to the right or upwards from LP_1 to LP_2 (because of an increase in the level of income) the rate interest rises from OR_1 to OR_2. This is illustrated as follows.

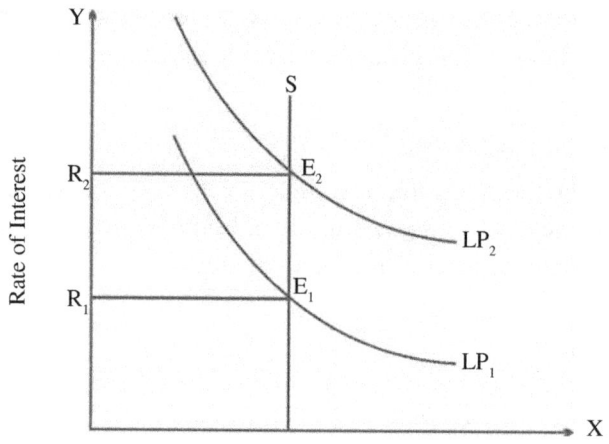

Demand for and Supply of Money

Figure 6.18: Changes in demand for money

In the above figure (Figure 6.18) the equilibrium point shifts from E_1 to E_2.

Changes in Supply of Money

With liquidity preference of the consumers remaining constant, an increase in the supply of money by the monetary authorities from $S_1 S_1$ to $S_2 S_2$ leads to *a* decline in the rate of interest from OR_1 or OR_2. This is illustrated as follows.

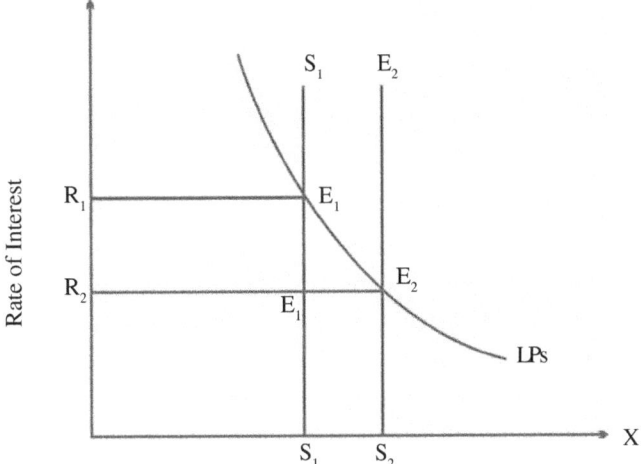

Demand for and Supply of Money

Figure 6.19 : Changes in supply of money

In the above diagram (Figure 6.19) the equilibrium points shift from E_1 to E_2. Thus, in the Keynesian theory of interest, interest is a purely monetary phenomenon determined by the demand for money and supply of money.

6.5 PROFIT

Production is the result of collective efforts of Lansd labour capital entrepreneur and organisation. The reward paid for the entrepjeneurial skill is called profit. This reward is the residual sum because after making payment to all the factors of production except share of entrepreneur for his services. This remuneration of entrepreneur may be positive as well as negative. Itit is positive there will be profit and when it is negative it will be lass.

Meaning and Definitions

Profit has been defined by different economists. Some of the definition are given below.

Prof. Schumpeter has defined *"Profit is the reward for the work of entrepreneurial ability or it is a payment of risks uncertainties and innovations. "*
Introduces a fourth category of sacrifice in the productive activities of man in a dynamic world. This category is risk taking or uncertainty bearing.

Prof. Paul A. Samuel ton has rightly pointed out *"What is profit? Economists do not always agree on the answer. A graduate student recently checked over a number of modern text books and came up with fourteen different answers."*

Salient features or profit

Following are the salient features of profit.
i)   Profit is a residual income.

ii) Higher the risk higher will be the profit.

iii) Profit is uncertain and indeterminate.

iv) Profit may be positive zero or negative

v) Profit has feature of fluctuations and it varies from one period to another.

Concepts of Profit

There are several concepts of profits. They are discussed below.

i) Gross profit : It is also called total profit. It is the residual income received by an entrepreneur when we exclude, total explicit costs. From total revenue of a firm. Explicit costs consist of the costs of raw material electricity charges, reward for the factors of production and depreciation -allowance, insurance premium etc. From the financial accounting point of view what is received, after deducting the direct costs from the total revenue is called gross profit. The gross profit can be calculated from the following fonnula.

Gross Profit = Economic Profit + Implicit Cost + Monopoly Profits + Windfall Profit

Or

Total Revenue – Total Explicit costs. From the financial accounting point of view.

Gross Profit = Total Revenue – Total Direct Costs

ii) Net profit : It is also called economic profit. Net profit is the reward paid to the entrepreneur for taking risks, uncertainly bearing and new innovations in the process of production. Prof. Thomas has rightly pointed out that net profit is the reward for taking risk paid to the entrepreneur only and the work of entrepreneurs cannot be undertaken by other factors of production. Thus, net profit or economic profit is the residual income occurred to the entrepreneur after making provisions for implicit and explicit costs from the total revenue. It can be calculated by the following formula.

Net Profit = Total Revenue - Explicit Cost – Implicit Cost

From the financial accounting point of view.

Net Profit = Total Revenue – Direct Costs – Indirect Costs.

Thus, net profit has following elements.

a) The payments for taking risk.

b) The reward for various innovations introduced by the entrepreneur.

c) The reward for the co-ordination among different factors of production.

d) Remuneration to the owned factors of production.

e) Depreciation and maintains charges.

f) Insurance charges and incidental charges.

g) Extra personal gain may be in the form of monopoly gains and windfall gains.

Theories of Profits

i) Dynamic Theory of Profits

The dynamic theory of profits has been developed by an American economist, Prof. J. B. Clark. He is of the opinion that profits arise only in a dynamic society and they do not arise in a static society. The static society is characterised by the absence of profits because in such a society it is always equal to the selling price. In such case, there can be no profits beyond wages for the routine work of supervision.

According to J.B. Clark, a dynamic society is one in which changes occur. These are the changes in the following factors.

i) Population
ii) Consumer behaviour
iii) Stock of capital
iv) Methods of production
v) Invention of new techniques
vi) Forms of industrial establishment;
vii) Wants of the consumers.

These dynamic changes cause difference between price and cost. Such difference is known as profit. Therefore, according to this theory, profit is a result of change. Such change occurs only in a dynamic society and not in the static society.

Therefore, profits arise only in a dynamic society. Entrepreneurs in a static society earn only the wages of general superintendence and the prices of factors supplied by them. Hence, dynamic changes are responsible for the emergence of profits.

We all live in a dynamic world which is characterised by change. Some changes are constantly taking place in our society. Therefore, profits arise in the society in which we live which is called the dynamic society. In brief, profits occurs only in a dynamic society.

Criticisms

This theory has been criticised on the following points.

i) Dynamic theory of profits explains the difference between profits and wages. But it is criticized on the ground that there is no difference between the wages of an entrepreneur and his profits.

ii) This theory has been criticised because it fails to determine the size of profits.

iii) Dynamic theory of profits given by Clark ignores profit as *a* reward for risk- taking. Critics point out that we can never ignore the risk element while determining profits.

iv) This theory has been criticised because it gives a poor explanation of the dynamic society. It explains only few components of a dynamic society. In reality, there are so many other changes which occur in a dynamic society but which were ignored by J.B. Clark.

v) It is not correct to say that profit arises only due to the changes occurring in a society. Profit is earned also due to ability and due to other managerial activities. So the dynamic theory of profits gives a poor explanation of the origin and nature of profits.

ii) Innovation Theory of Profit

Joseph Schumpeter has developed the innovation theory of profit. His theory of profit is more or less a skin to the dynamic theory of profit.

Joseph Schumpeter's theory of profit attributes *"Occurrence of profit to the introduction of innovations in the production process or sale of product by the entrepreneur."*

In common usage innovation refers so some form of technological progress or resource discovery. Schumpeter, however, attached a wider meaning to this concept. According to him. "This concept covers the following cases.

i) The introduction of a new goods.

ii) The introduction of a new method of production.

iii) The opening of a new market

iv) The conquest of new source of supply of raw materials, of half manufactured goods.

v) The carrying out of the new organisation of any industries like the creation of a monopoly position.

Meaning of Innovation

A new measure of policy designed by the entrepreneur to reduce costs of production or to increase the demand production or to increase the demand for his product is known as innovation.

Innovation may be divided into two broad categories.

i. Those innovations which reduce the cost of production: The cost of production may be reduced by the introduction of a new machine, new and cheaper techniques of production. Exploitation of a new source of raw material, new and better way of organising the firms etc.

ii. Those innovations which change the demand or utility function. The utility or demand may be increased by the introduction of a new product, a new design in the market, attractive and effective methods of advertisements, discovery of new markets for the product etc.

Meaning of Innovator

Innovator is a person who undertakes the risk of introducing the idea in mass commercial use. He is a person with vision, originality and drive. The entrepreneur is one who innovates Entrepreneurships and his Endeavour lies in introducing innovations. An entrepreneur may not be scientist who invents new products or processes but the man who successfully introduces them in the production process. The scientist or technician gets only a fixed sum or a percentage by way of royalty. The profit is due only to the entrepreneur.

The role of an entrepreneur is quite distinct from that of the capitalist. The entrepreneur innovates and does not undertake any risk. Risk taking is the function of a capitalist or the banks that provide credit. Thus profit is a reward for innovation rather than risk taking. An innovator is not always successful in his attempts. But when he succeeds he is rewarded in the form of profit.

Profits are of temporary nature. The entrepreneur who innovates earns abnormal profits for a short period. Soon other entrepreneurs compete for profit in the same manner. He will make another innovation.

In a dynamic world innovation in one field leads to changes in related fields. The emergence of motor car industry may in turn stimulate new investments in the construction of highways, rubber, tyres, and petroleum products. Profits are thus causes and effects of innovation. The interest of profit leads entrepreneur to innovate and innovations leads to profits. Thus profit has a tendency to appear, disappear. Profits are caused by innovation and 'disappear by imitation. According to Schumpeter innovational profit is thus, never permanent. It is, therefore, different from other incomes such as rent, wages and interest.

These are the permanent incomes arising under all circumstances. Profit, on the other hand, is a temporary surplus resulting from innovation.

In the opinion of Schumpeter the real function of the entrepreneur is to introduce innovations in business. It is the innovations which yield him profit.

Criticism

The theory is criticised as follows :

i) According to critics, Schumpeter's theory is nothing else than the uncertainty theory, for innovation are one of the causes of uncertainly, although a deliberately created uncertainty.

ii) This theory concentrates only on innovations, which is only of the many function of the entrepreneur.

iii) The theory does not consider profit as the reward for risk-taking. According to Schumpeter it is the capitalist not the entrepreneur who undertake risk. In reality it is the entrepreneur, not the capitalist who takes risk.

iv) This theory has ignored the importance of uncertainty bearing which is one of the factors that determines profit.

v) It is an incomplete theory because it has failed to explain all the factors influencing profit.

vi) The theory presents a narrow view of the function of the entrepreneurs. He not only introduces innovation but he is equally responsible for proper organization of the business. As such profit is not merely due to innovation. It is also due to organizational work performed by the entrepreneur.

vii) The theory ignores the windfall gains and losses.

iii) Risk and Uncertainty - Theory of Profits

Prof. F. H. Knight made an improvement over the risk bearing theory and presented a refined version called the "Uncertainty bearing theory of profits. According to Prof. Knight. There is intense association between profit and uncertainty. He held that entrepreneur's main function is not to take risks but is to bear uncertainties.

Prof. Knight has divided risks in to two parts in order to clearly differentiate between risks and uncertainly.

i) *Insurable Risk :* Prof. Knight pointed out that there are some risks which can be foreseen. In other words, we can make a rough estimate about some risks. Such risks can be avoided by insuring them. Examples of such risk are fire, accidents etc.' Insurance companies can compensate them at a rate of premium. The premium paid for covering such risks becomes a part of cost of production. So there is no uncertainty borne by the entrepreneur in such risks.

ii) *Non-Insurable Risks :* There are some risks which cannot be foreseen. There are changes in fashions, fluctuations in price level and changes in the customs and habits of the people. Such risks cannot be insured.. Prof. Knight pointed out that profit is the reward for such unforeseen risks .which cannot be insured or avoided.

Prof. Knight pointed out that the entrepreneur may have to bear uncertainties of the following kinds.

a) Uncertainty in the market conditions of the product from the consumer's side.

b) Uncertain behaviour of the competitors.

c) Uncertainty regarding technical changes in machines and equipment.

d) Uncertainties regarding trade cycles.

e) Uncertainty regarding intervention by the Government.

In this way, Knight emphasised uncertainty - bearing as the main function of the entrepreneur for which he gets profits..Unless a certain return is expected, no entrepreneur will come forth to bear the uncertainty involved. He said that even under condition of perfect competition when total product is exhausted after paying the factors of production, an entrepreneur earn positive profits.

Criticism of Knight's Theory

Knight's theory has been widely discussed and criticise by many economists. The main shortcomings of the theory pointed out that different economists from time to time have been listed below:

i) The most fundamental criticism of the theory is directed at its attempt to raise uncertainty-bearing to the status of a full-fledged factor of production. The critics point out that if we consider profit as an inducement to bear uncertainty, it implies that there is connection between the level of profit and uncertainty. But no such connection exists.

ii) Profit is not simply the result of uncertainty bearing. This theory does not give any place to such functions as co-ordination, decision making and supervision.

iii) Not applicable to joint stock companies : The entrepreneurial functions are divided among shareholders, directors and managers of the company. It is not clear in this theory as to who bears uncertainty.

Hawtey's Risk Theory of Profits

The risk theory of profits has been developed by an American economist. F.B. Hawley and supported by Marshall.

According to this theory, *"Profit arises on account of the risk undertaken by the entrepreneur."* Or *"Risk-taking as the function of the entrepreneur. For this purpose, he gets profits as an inducement"*. Hawley opined that work of the entrepreneur involves many risks. He explained four types of risks which are undertaken by the entrepreneur.

i) *Replacement risk :* Replacement risk is also called depreciation. It is calculable. It is added in to the costs.

ii) *Obsolescence risk :* Obsolescence Risk is not measurable because it is not always possible to anticipate technical progress.

iii) *Risk proper :* Risk proper is risk of marketability of the product.

iv) *Uncertainty risk :* Uncertainty risk is regard to unforeseen factors.

Entrepreneur bears all these risk in the hope of earning profits. Nobody can stay in production without hoping for profits. So profits may be called 'costs of staying in business' so profit is a reward for risk-taking.

Criticism

The risk-bearing theory of profits has been criticised on the following grounds.

i) This theory considers profits as a reward for taking risks. But critics point out that profit is a mixed income they arise not only due to risk-taking but also from the ability, managerial powers and bargaining powers of the entrepreneur.

ii) Some critics point out that "Profits arise not because risks are borne by entrepreneurs but because the superior entrepreneurs, are able to reduce them."

iii) Prof. Knight pointed out that profits arise not due to all risks. Some risks can be foreseen. They can be insured. So they are covered. Profits occur due to only those risks which are unforeseen, unpredictable and not insurable.

iv) It is wrong to believe that there is a proportionate relationship between risk and profits as was believed by Hawley. In reality, profit and risks are not rigidly related to each other.

v) The expectations of the entrepreneur play an important role in the choice of his production. These are short term and long term expectations. Both these expectations affect profits. This theory is not clear on the role of expectations.

vi) The theory does not help us in determining the profit share in macro distribution. It only explains the determination of profits in a micro sense. For determining the share of profits in macro distribution, the classical theory of profit is more helpful.

We can say about Knight's theory that it wrongly assumes profits to be only due to uncertainties. Uncertainties arise only due to changes. So if no changes occur, no profit will be eared.

EXERCISE

1. Define marginal physical productivity, marginal value product, marginal revenue productivity and Average Revenue productivity.
2. Critically examine Marginal productivity theory of distribution.
3. What are the assumptions of Marginal productivity theory of distribution.
4. What are the factors which influence supply of labour?
5. Discuss the loanable funds theory of interest.

6. Explain the Dynamic Theory of Profits.
7. Explain the Innovation theory of profits.
8. Critically examine the marginal productivity theory of distribution.
9. Discuss the Ricardian theory of rent.
10. Explain the modern theory of Rent.
11. Explain the liquidity preference theory of interest.
12. Discuss the risk and uncertainty bearing theory of profits.

References

1. Economics – Samuelson P. A. and Nordhaus W. D. TataMcgrew Hill Publishing Co. Ltd. N.Delhi.

2. A text Book of Economic Theory – Stonier A. W. and Hague D. C. Longman Green and Co. London

3. Business Economics – V. G. Mankar, Macmillan India Ltd. N. Delhi.

4. Vyavasaik Arth Shastra (Sukshm) Dr. T. G. Gite, Atharv Publication. Pune

5. Modern Micro Economics – Theory and Applications H.L. Ahujna S. Chand and Co Ltd. N Delhi.

6. Business Economics – Dr. Girija Shankar – Atharv Publication, Pune.

7. Principals of Economics – N.Gregory Mankiw 6th edition 2012 Cengage learning india pvt ltd Delhi.

8. Understanding Microeconomics- Robert L. Helibroner and Lester C. Thurow. Prentice Hall International Inc. London.

9. Micro Economic Theory An Analytical Approach – J M Joshi and R. Joshi Wishwa Prakashan (Division of Wiley Eastern Limited) N. Delhi.

10. Business & Managerial Economics (in the global Context) Sampat Mukherjee. New Central Book Agency, Calcutta.

11. Micro Economics Theory and Application D.N.Dwivedi Second Edition PEARSON.

References

1. Economics – Samuelson P. A. and Nordhaus W. D. TataMcgrew Hill Publishing Co. Ltd. N.Delhi.

2. A text Book of Economic Theory – Stonier A. W. and Hague D. C. Longman Green and Co. London

3. Business Economics – V. G. Mankar, Macmillan India Ltd. N. Delhi.

4. Vyavasaik Arth Shastra (Sukshm) Dr. T. G. Gite, Atharv Publication. Pune

5. Modern Micro Economics – Theory and Applications H.L. Ahujna S. Chand and Co Ltd. N Delhi.

6. Business Economics – Dr. Girija Shankar – Atharv Publication, Pune.

7. Principals of Economics – N.Gregory Mankiw 6th edition 2012 Cengage learning india pvt ltd Delhi.

8. Understanding Microeconomics- Robert L. Helibroner and Lester C. Thurow. Prentice Hall International Inc. London.

9. Micro Economic Theory An Analytical Approach – J M Joshi and R. Joshi Wishwa Prakashan (Division of Wiley Eastern Limited) N. Delhi.

10. Business & Managerial Economics (in the global Context) Sampat Mukherjee. New Central Book Agency, Calcutta.

11. Micro Economics Theory and Application D.N.Dwivedi Second Edition PEARSON.